Graymarsh pulled Sarah into his arms. His face was pale. His voice shook. "I thought I'd lost you forever." And, unable to adequately express the horror and bleakness of that prospect, he abandoned the attempt and held her closer, then met her upturned lips with his.

No sooner was that contact made than Sarah soared again. She was light-headed—she was spinning—she was flying—it was glorious, beyond belief. Ballooning was indeed an experience she would not have missed for the world.

Miss Romney Flies Too High

Marian Devon

FAWCETT CREST • NEW YORK

A Fawcett Crest Book
Published by Ballantine Books
Copyright © 1986 by Marian Pope Rettke

All rights reserved under International and Pan-American Copyright Conventions. Published in the United States by Ballantine Books, a division of Random House, Inc., New York, and simultaneously in Canada by Random House of Canada Limited, Toronto.

Library of Congress Catalog Card Number: 86-90880

ISBN: 0-449-20844-3

All the characters in this book are fictitious and any resemblance to actual persons, living or dead, is purely coincidental.

Manufactured in the United States of America

First Edition: July 1986

for Leslie and the Gordons

Chapter One

*Lord Petherbridge lay dying—once again. But if the an*gel of death was indeed hovering, as the two nephews who had dutifully obeyed the summons to attend his lordship's final hours were prone to doubt, that dread messenger could possibly have been put off by the invalid's scowling countenance. The old gentleman was propped up by a mountainous pile of pillows against the headboard of a mahogany four-poster bed. His nightcap was askew on his puckered forehead. His bushy gray eyebrows beetled over protuberant pale blue eyes that glared at the young men who had been attending him for the better part of an hour.

"What's keeping Gray?" his lordship snapped. "I said I wanted the three of you here at two o'clock. It's almost four."

As if to be perverse, the clock in the hallway whirred a bit and then struck hollowly. "It's just three, sir." The Honorable Randolph Milbanke had taken the trouble to count, in defense of his absent brother. His tabulation earned him an offended stare from his great-uncle and a wicked, if swift, smile from his older cousin.

"Sit down, will you, Randolph." His lordship waved impatiently toward the carved and gilt armchair that the lanky young man in riding coat and buckskins had recently vacated. "You're pacing like a caged beast in the tower menagerie. I'll say this much for Gerard, he ain't fidgety." He bestowed an almost benign look upon the exquisite sprawled in a wing chair in front of the Adam fireplace—not for warmth, since the grate was empty and the month was June, but because the chair happened to be placed so and he had seen no need to expend the energy it would take to shift it.

Mr. Gerard Langford, elegantly clad in bottle-green long-tailed coat, champagne breeches, and shiny Hessians, yawned lazily and stared at his cousin through his quizzing glass. "Uncle's right, you know. One might suspect you're uneasy over Gray's defection. The sentiment shows commendable loyalty, I suppose, but a deplorable lack of self-interest, I must say." He smiled mockingly at Randolph.

No one, least of all his cousin, would have accused Mr. Langford of such a lack. The mistake that casual acquaintances often did make was to be led astray by some carefully cultivated mannerisms into writing him off as merely a fop. Fooled by the conjurer's trick of diversion, they noted the handsome face and the artfully curled fair hair and overlooked the muscular shoulders under the Weston coat and the calculating look that lurked behind the lazy azure eyes. His cousin Randolph was not so easily deceived. "Gray ain't defected, Gerry. He'll be here." He gave the other a challenging stare and obediently resumed his seat.

''Shows a want of feeling.'' There was injury in his lordship's tone. ''When a man sends a message to town to say he's dying and wants his family at his side—well, he certainly expects punctuality. Could've already breathed me last as far as Graymarsh knows.''

''Oh, I don't think that Gray expects . . .'' Randolph's disclaimer sputtered and died under his uncle's glare. Gerard's muffled chuckle was its death knell. Randolph reddened to the roots of his Brutus-styled brown hair. But once again fraternal loyalty overcame self-interest. The usually amiable boyish face set stubbornly. ''Since this ain't the first time we've been sent for, sir, I expect that Gray hopes for the best. Or''—Randolph Milbanke clutched at straws—''more likely, he never got your message.''

''Oh, he got it all right.'' Mr. Langford casually picked an imaginary piece of lint from the sleeve his valet had brushed lovingly and unnecessarily a few hours before. ''Saw him at White's. Said so.'' He met his cousin's indignant gaze with an ingenuous smile.

''Well, then, he'll be here,'' Randolph said staunchly, just as the sound of metal wheels on gravel and heavy, plodding hoofbeats came drifting through the open windows. ''What in the—'' He broke off.

''I would hazard a guess that the laggard has arrived,'' his cousin replied lazily.

''Can't be.'' Randolph was on his feet, though, hurrying toward a window that overlooked the carriage drive. He leaned perilously far out of it. ''It is him! My God!''

His shocked tone was enough to spur his languid cousin into action. Gerard followed Randolph to the window and peered through his quizzing glass past the other's shoulder. ''My God,'' he echoed softly.

''What is it? What's going on?'' His lordship's voice boomed with surprising vigor as he sat upright. ''Somebody tell me what's going on!''

''Lord Graymarsh has finally arrived, sir,'' Mr. Langford drawled as he turned away from the window and strolled back to collapse once again into his chair, heaving a weary sigh. "In a horse cart. Perched on a load of straw. Driven by a rustic."

"Wha—wha—" His uncle's prominent eyes protruded even farther as he sputtered, "Don't bam me, boy, just because I'm dying. What would Graymarsh be doing on a load of hay?"

"Curst if I know." The other yawned. "But like you, I await the explanation with bated breath."

The wait was not a long one. Lord Petherbridge continued to sit bolt upright; the Honorable Randolph Milbanke stood rooted in mid-chamber, staring at the door; and even Mr. Langford exerted himself so far as to shift his chair a fraction to provide a better view of the entryway. They remained in a tableau while the sound of hurrying footsteps taking the stairs two at a time echoed down the hall. The chamber door opened a second later and Winfield Milbanke, the sixth Baron of Graymarsh, strode in.

It was not immediately apparent that he and Randolph were brothers. He was half a head shorter than the nineteen-year-old, who had shot to an amazing height during the past year. And while he possessed only a medium-size frame and trim figure, he was well-muscled and filled out in contrast to his brother. His hair was darker, almost black, and there was nothing boyish about his face. In fact, the high cheekbones, angular jaw, and slightly hawkish nose made his countenance appear forbidding at times. This effect was slightly softened by clear gray eyes and a charming smile, which was now directed at his uncle.

"Oh, good. You're looking quite the thing. I had hoped so. Though that doesn't wash as an excuse for being late. I must seem positively rag-mannered. I beg your pardon for it."

Lord Graymarsh's terminology could have been called

into question. His uncle, while obviously not expiring, did not, however, look "quite the thing." In point of fact, his mouth was gaping in a fishlike manner—the resemblance heightened by his popping eyes—as he took in the appearance of the late arrival.

At the best of times, the sixth Baron of Graymarsh could lay no claim to dandyism. But he was, as a rule, quietly up to snuff. And if not precisely fastidious, neither was he careless. At least that had been the case. At the moment, however, his lordship's gray riding coat was flecked with mud, and there was a large triangular tear in the left sleeve. His buckskins were even muddier than his coat, while his top boots, in spite of some efforts to clean them off, had obviously been wading in the muck. Here and there, wisps of straw clung to his apparel.

"Gray— What on earth!" Lord Graymarsh's brother gasped while at the same time Lord Petherbridge gave tongue. "They said you came here in a hay cart." Despite the tangible evidence clinging to his nephew's clothing, his voice was rich with disbelief.

"I'm afraid I did, sir." Petherbridge's favorite nephew walked over to the four-poster and looked ruefully at his uncle. "It wasn't my intention. I left from outside London by balloon, you see."

"You did what?" his uncle roared, while his brother gasped and exclaimed, "Oh, I say, did you?" and his cousin shook his head despairingly.

"Came in a balloon!" Lord Petherbridge's voice dropped a bit in volume but retained its disbelief.

"Didn't you know, Uncle?" Gerard drawled. "It's his latest start. My scientific cousin has forsaken the steam engine for balloons. Really, Gray," he said with a sigh, "why can't you be content being a bang-up-to-the-nines whip like anybody else? Balloons! Terribly bad form. Not at all the thing."

Lord Petherbridge seemed of the selfsame mind. "You

came from London in a balloon?'' From the heightened ferocity of his frown, this sin far outweighed tardiness. ''After I'd sent word to you I was on me deathbed, you took a balloon to get here? Why, the public coach would have been more respectable. I must say, Winfield, I'm disappointed in you. Wouldn't have expected such rackety behavior on your part. From Randolph maybe, but not you. You'll soon be thirty. Besides, it ain't respectful at any age to come to somebody's deathbed by balloon. Shows a want of serious feeling.''

Mr. Langford seemed to be enjoying his cousin's setdown, while Randolph looked offended by the reference to himself. Only the chief recipient of the old gentleman's displeasure appeared unaffected. ''Well, actually,'' he explained amiably, ''at daybreak it seemed quite a good idea. All the conditions were favorable for a flight. I should have been able to come down somewhere in the vicinity. But unfortunately the wind shifted and I was carried miles out of my way and wound up in a bog. By the time I'd rescued myself and the balloon—and walked for several miles before the farmer's cart came along . . . Well, instead of stealing a march on my brother and my cousin, I've kept you waiting. Again, I do beg your pardon for it.'' His smile took in the other two as well as the old gentleman.

''I could've been dead by the time you got here,'' the latter said petulantly.

''*He* could've been dead, coming by balloon!'' Randolph protested.

''There was little chance of either.'' Because of his muddy clothes, Lord Graymarsh carefully avoided the upholstered furniture and pulled a spoon-backed chair with a cane bottom up close to the bed. ''Ballooning's not as dangerous as it's popularly conceived to be''—this was said to his brother as he sat down—''and, Uncle, I presume that there's something besides dying on your mind.''

Randolph gasped at his brother's forthrightness and braced himself for the explosion that was sure to follow. But surprisingly, the old gentleman appeared less angry than embarrassed. "Cried wolf too often, have I?"

"Well . . ." His nephew crossed his muddy top boots at the ankles. "You do seem to find it necessary to take to your bed when you want us here on business," he offered mildly.

"There's a good reason for it," Petherbridge replied.

"I supposed there might be."

"It's your aunt."

"Oh. Our aunt. I see."

"No, you don't," his uncle corrected, and Lord Graymarsh's expression acknowledged the accuracy of the hit. "I think the world and all of your aunt." Lord Petherbridge fixed each nephew in turn with a belligerent gaze as if daring them to contradict his statement.

They had no intention of doing so. Not only politeness interfered. They all knew that this statement was true, even if they didn't pretend to understand it. A care-for-nothing and member of the Regent's raffish set, Petherbridge had, in his late middle age, begun a relentless pursuit of their do-gooder aunt Augusta. And when she had finally consented to abandon her advanced maiden state and marry him, it had been the *on-dit* of the ton for an entire season. But no one, least of all the lady's nephews, had doubted for a moment that it was a love match. Miss Milbanke was, of course, quite well-to-do. But Lord Petherbridge was a nabob. And during the ensuing years, unlike many grand but short-lived passions, their attachment had increased, underscoring the truth of the principle that opposites attract.

"I think the world of your aunt," his lordship repeated for extra emphasis, "and the last thing I want to do is cause her grief. That's why I had to send word to you that I was dying."

If the young men found some incongruity in that statement, they didn't say so. All three were, figuratively at least, on the edges of their chairs. "The thing is, you see," Lord Petherbridge said solemnly, "Augusta thinks I just want to say me last good-byes. But the truth is, I've important business that needs discussion. I brought you here to talk about my will."

If he had thought to drop a bombshell, his lordship was disappointed. Lord Graymarsh waited politely for him to continue. Randolph nodded as in confirmation of a fixed idea. Mr. Langford carefully inspected his manicured nails. When it became apparent that no one chose to comment, Lord Petherbridge forged ahead. "I think you've guessed that I'd always intended the three of you to share in what I leave behind me." He paused. No one replied. But what, in point of fact, they might have said was that no one had to guess. Once it had become established that his lordship's marriage was not to be blessed with progeny, the heirless nobleman had been quite vocal. He let it be widely known that his wife's nephews—the two sons of her brother, the fifth Baron of Graymarsh, and the only son of a sister improvident enough to have married a handsome ne'er-do-well to disoblige her family—stood to inherit the bulk of his estate. "Of course," his lordship continued, "I hadn't quite decided on the particulars, like who'd get the hall." He looked around him fondly as if he could see through the bedchamber walls to the rest of his palatial residence. "That put me in a quandary. Gray has his own seat and might prefer to live there. Gerard ain't got much taste for country life."

"Oh, I say!" For once the dandy was jolted from his lethargy while his younger cousin broke into a grin. The grin faded as the old man continued. "And Randolph's too much of a green 'un. Can't say what sort of a landlord he may be. So that part's never been quite settled in my mind." He mused over the problem once more for old times' sake. "But never mind all that." He jerked himself back into the present. "It don't matter now how my mind was running when I led you to think you'd all inherit. Because the thing is, I've changed it. That's why I called the three of you down here."

He had already claimed their attention. Now the atmosphere fairly crackled with suspense. Even Mr. Langford had dropped his pose and was looking at his uncle warily. Randolph wore a worried frown. Lord Graymarsh was the only one whose interest seemed merely academic and detached.

"It's nothing personal," Lord Petherbridge assured them. "I couldn't think any more of you if you were me own flesh and blood and not Augusta's. But that's the point, you see."

All three young men looked equally bemused, but it was Graymarsh who asked politely, "What point exactly, sir?"

"That you ain't me own flesh and blood." His lordship frowned at the other's denseness. "You see, I've a mind to leave the hall and most of what I've got to me own offspring. Oh, there'll still be a bequest for each of you. But nothing like you've been led to expect. Which may be a bit hard for you to understand at your age. But it takes a man that way as he gets older. A man wants his own flesh and blood to follow in his footsteps. So that's what I've decided. Hope you'll come to understand in time."

The three were totally bewildered now, searching their uncle's face for other signs of dementia. It was young Randolph who blurted, "Surely you ain't thinking of setting up your nursery at this late date!"

He was squelched by a withering, "At Augusta's age? Don't be sap-skulled." But then his lordship's scowl turned into an expression close to embarrassment. "The thing is—and, mind you, if you breathe a word of what I'm going to say outside these walls, you'll be cut out of me will entirely—that part's already been taken care of."

"You mean you already have a child?" Again, the indiscretion came from Randolph. He turned beet-red.

"I mean I already have a daughter." There was pride now mixed in with the embarrassment. "She ain't a child, though. She's twenty-one. Or maybe twenty-two. Can't be sure now. But anyhow, she's what I've brought you down here to talk about. You see, it's been growing on me gradually for a long time now that she's the one I want to settle the bulk of my fortune on. A man likes to think of his own bloodline continuing on his land, don't you know," he explained apologetically once more. "But the thing is, I don't want to upset Augusta. It would go hard on most childless women, I collect, having their husband's by-blow sprung on 'em after he was dead and gone. But Augusta . . ." He shuddered. "Well, it just don't bear thinking on."

The stunned young men were quick to see his point. There were some women who were prepared to blink at the fact that their husbands had produced progeny on the wrong side of the blanket. Lady Petherbridge was not one of their number.

"So you see, even though I've always wanted to name me daughter Sarah as me heir, I didn't like to cause Augusta grief. But the other evening over port it came to me—like one of those revelations you always hear of—how I could work the thing with no one the wiser, least of all Augusta." He beamed at his nephews, awaiting congratulations for his brilliance. When none was forthcoming, he gave them the same kind of look they all remembered receiving from disappointed schoolmasters. "Don't you get the point, lads? I'm leaving the hall and the bulk of my fortune to whichever of you marries little Sarah."

"I beg your pardon?" Gerard Langford didn't bother with his quizzing glass. The stare he bent upon his uncle was intense enough. "I'm not at all sure I heard you right. Or if I did hear right, I'm not sure I understand."

"Well, you ought to have done. Didn't I just explain it? I can't name me bastard"—all three young men flinched at such forthrightness—"in the will. It would upset Augusta. Not to mention giving the gossip-mongers a juicy bone to gnaw. So I'm leaving the lion's share of me fortune to one of you. After all, that's what everybody expects me to do. The thing is, the one that gets it has to marry Sarah. Then that will settle everything right and tight."

The old man leaned back against his pillows and surveyed his nephews. His look of self-congratulation was not reflected on their faces. There was a long, awkward silence. Mr. Langford recovered first. "And just how do you propose we, er, set about this, ah, project?" he drawled.

His uncle snorted. "Coming it a bit strong, ain't you? Happen to know there's nobody more in the petticoat line than you are, Gerry. Why, there was one particular little ladybird in Covent Garden, I recall, when you weren't even as old as Randolph here. And now, if I can believe even half the stories—"

"I think what my cousin means," Graymarsh interposed, "is that you haven't told us anything about your daughter yet. Except that she's called Sarah and one of us is supposed to marry her."

"And that she's twenty-one. Or twenty-two," his brother offered for the record.

"For starters, where do we find the, uh, quarry?" Gerard inquired.

Randolph added, "What does she look like?"

"Most likely like her mother." Lord Petherbridge chose to deal with the second question first. "Girls generally do." Involuntarily, all three stared at their host's bulbous nose and bulging eyes as they mulled over this novel theory of heredity. "Oh, how I hope so," Mr. Langford opined, sotto voce, as Lord Petherbridge continued. "Best as I can recall, her mother was a prime 'un. Would have had to've been,'' he added reflectively.

''Don't you remember?'' Randolph sounded shocked.

''Just told you. It was twenty-one—or twenty-two, I ain't quite sure which—years ago. Before I met your aunt Augusta, anyhow. Besides, a cove can't be expected to remember every bit of muslin from his salad days.'' He glared at Randolph.

''Except that this particular dalliance seems to have left a rather lasting impression.'' Mr. Langford helped himself to snuff from a silver box.

''Naturally, I've provided for the girl.'' Lord Petherbridge felt pushed onto the defensive. ''Not handsomely, mind you. But well enough. Back then I didn't want to give her ideas above her station. Never expected not to have offspring in wedlock, don't you see. But I did see to it that she went to school. So she shouldn't disgrace the one of you who gets her. Besides, she's an actress. Should be able to carry off being a lady. Sort of thing they're trained to do.''

''An actress!'' Randolph gasped. ''One of us is expected to marry an actress?''

''I'll admit it don't sound quite the thing at first,'' his lordship conceded. ''But when you stop to think on it, it ain't all that unusual. It's always happening—actresses sweeping coves off their feet, I mean. I've known any number of men in the first circles to be completely besotted about actresses. Why the Regent himself—''

''Yes, but His Highness never actually married his Perdita,'' Lord Graymarsh offered.

''Well, he couldn't, could he? Stands to reason. The crown and all. And, well, I'll grant you, in our world it is more the usual thing to offer a carte blanche. But still, this won't be the first time a gentleman was knocked off his feet by an actress and lost his head enough to marry her. Oh, you'll set the tongues awagging for a while. But the gossip-mongers will soon move on to something else. Always do. And then everything will be right and tight."

"I don't wish to be indelicate, sir," Mr. Langford drawled, "but since you don't seem to know what your daughter looks like, what makes you think the thing will wash? Take Gray there, for instance. You must be aware that he's the prime catch of the marriage mart. Every diamond of the first water who comes along casts out lures for him. Been doing it for years. Not to mention all the encroaching mamas who fling their daughters at his head. And young Randolph, while far more callow and a lot less moneyed, is personable enough—for a mere stripling—and certainly well born enough to snare himself a, uh, respectable heiress. As for myself, well, modesty prevents my comment. The point is, your daughter would have to be something out of the ordinary to make such a flagrant misalliance believable."

"No, she wouldn't." This flat statement was loaded with conviction. "No accounting for tastes when it comes to falling in love. Just look around you. Very few love matches make sense. Take your aunt and me. Think we didn't know we were a nine-days' wonder?"

"I take your point," his nephew remarked dryly.

"Besides, ain't I been telling you to overlook the gossip? The thing to keep in mind is that I want me own daughter to inherit while me wife stays none the wiser. And having one of you marry the girl is the way to do it. I don't mind saying it's a dashed fine scheme."

"Yes, I can see that from your point of view it's a solution worthy of Solomon." Graymarsh settled back in his chair, moving from his recent position on its edge. "But it must have occurred to you that the three of us might not be quite so enthusiastic."

"No, it didn't. I may not be one of your intellectual coves, but I do know human nature. There's a fortune at stake here. At least one of you will come up to scratch.

And one's all I need. Now I've told you me terms. All I have to add is that me girl's appearing with a traveling company at Portsmouth Theatre. You can take it from there.'' Lord Petherbridge reached up and gave the bellpull a tug. "Oh, I almost forgot. There is one other thing. I ain't getting any younger. And one of these days when I take to me deathbed there'll be no getting back up again. So I'm giving you just six months to fix your interest with me Sarah. If one of you hasn't done the thing by that time, well, I'll put my Yorkshire cousins in the field. One way or another, I mean to have me flesh and blood at Pether Hall.''

An ancient butler, who looked as if he, not his employer, should be recumbent, answered the bell's summons. "Me nephews are just leaving, Mason. Give 'em a glass of port in the library if they want it.'' Lord Petherbridge settled his nightcap and fluffed up his pillows. "It's past time for me nap,'' he remarked petulantly. "All your fault, Gray. Traveling by balloon. Of all the havey-cavey things. Wouldn't've been done in me day, I can tell you.''

The three candidates for the hand of Lord Petherbridge's by-blow did opt for port. They seemed to be in need of a restorative. When Mason had deposited a decanter and glasses on the mahogany pedestal library table and then departed, there was a few minutes' silence while each drained his glass more quickly than gentility decreed. Randolph was the first to find his voice. He gazed about him at the rich paneling of the room; at the floor-to-ceiling shelves filled with handsomely bound, if seldom touched, rows and rows of books; at the Turner painting hanging over the black marble chimney piece. Then he said, "I think I'm going to like living here.''

His brother strangled on his port. His cousin raised an eyebrow. "Wouldn't you call such an observation a bit premature?''

"Why, no. Stands to reason I'll inherit. I'm the only serious candidate."

The other reemployed his quizzing glass. "The *only* candidate? Whatever gave you such a maggoty idea?"

"What's maggoty about it? Gray's already as rich as Croesus and doesn't have to dangle after any kind of heiress. And a high stickler like you ain't about to marry some cit actress. My God, a provincial player! Why, it ain't like she was at least from Covent Garden or Drury Lane. Portsmouth!" He wrinkled his nose. "And heaven knows what she'll look like, let alone how rag-mannered she's bound to be. And it ain't as though you're desperate. It's the latest *on-dit* in town that old Scriven's widow's mad for you. Besides, Aunt Augusta's bound to leave you something. You're her favorite."

"True," his cousin answered softly. "But have you stopped to think that both those ladies' fortunes taken together don't even begin to touch our uncle's?"

"Maybe not. But his is a bird in the bush, don't you know. The widow's a sure thing."

"I don't think you'll make Gerard cry off with that kind of reasoning, little brother," Lord Graymarsh interposed. "When it comes to birds in bushes, don't overlook our cousin's most important trait. Gerry's a gambler, first and foremost. Can't resist a challenge. Don't take my word for it. Go have a look at White's betting book. Nobody's name appears with more regularity than his. Right, coz?"

Mr. Langford raised his glass in acknowledgment. He studied the other thoughtfully. "And how about you, Coz? Is your little brother right in thinking that you've no use for another fortune and will stick with your balloons and engines and God knows what else to give him a better run at our uncle's heiress?"

Graymarsh examined his crystal wineglass thoughtfully, perhaps looking for sediment in the vintage. The beginning of a smile played in his eyes. "I'm not sure myself, actually. I haven't quite decided. But I do believe that, just as in your case, my brother has overlooked my most important trait."

"Greed?" Mr. Langford asked politely.

"No." His lordship grinned. "Curiosity. Our uncle Petherbridge has made me very, very curious, Cousin."

Chapter Two

Miss Sarah Romney stood at the back of Portsmouth Theatre to count the house. The job was depressing but not difficult. A sweeping glance over the pit, boxes, and gallery sufficed to show that the place was only a quarter filled. Or three-fourths empty, she thought gloomily.

Not that Sarah was surprised. She'd shared none of her stepfather's conviction that the public would flock in droves to see Master Tidswell Romney. She'd done her part, however, to make it a success: going to prominent homes in town to sell subscriptions, doing a large woodcut for posters of a small Master Tidswell dressed in armor.

But the public in 1816 was not as taken with infant prodigies as they had been some ten years before when Master Betty had taken the London stage by storm and, hailed as the wonder of the age, had been presented to the king and queen. But the manager of the Romney Company of Players for some five years now had hoped to re-create the craze with his own offspring. His optimism was undeterred by the fact that Tidswell had none of the charm of a Master Betty or the talent of an Edmund Kean, once a "celebrated theatrical child" and now the star of Drury Lane. And to add to these other drawbacks, nature was about to deal Mr. Romney's hopes a cruel blow. Though still mercifully small for his age, at twelve Tidswell was rapidly phasing out of prodigy range. The thought caused Sarah to heave a heavy sigh.

"Oh, m'dear, did I not say so?" A voice spoke suddenly in her ear. "Our success is now assured."

Startled, Sarah turned to see if her late mother's husband had parted with his senses. The manager's appearance confirmed that dismal diagnosis. He was looking out over the near-empty auditorium, his ample face, forever amiable, now beaming; his hands gleefully washing each other, a gesture he'd often used to point up Shylock's greed. "I always knew my son would make our fortune. Did I not say so, Sarah?"

Sarah was looking at him anxiously. If rarely in accord with her stepfather's point of view, she was very fond of him. It distressed her now that, under the threat of losing his theatrical company, he might, in truth, be coming quite unhinged. "But Adolphus," she said gently, "there's hardly anybody here."

"Numbers! Pooh!" Mr. Romney dismissed the head count with the same airy wave he'd used as Claudius in *Hamlet*. "It isn't the quantity of the audience that ultimately matters, m'dear, when theatrical reputations are being made. It's the quality. Remember that," he added pontifically, rubbing his straining waistcoat, a Falstaff mannerism so overdone that a button had popped off. "Have you seen who's in the stage box?" he crowed.

Sarah had not. Indeed, from that vantage point it was all that she could do to see that the box was occupied. And the fact that it was hardly seemed to warrant Mr. Romney's degree of jubilation.

He explained, "There are three young gentlemen in it, m'dear. None of your yokels. Regular swells. Members of the ton. Types found at Covent Garden. Seen at Drury Lane. Used to the highest levels of performance. In evening dress. Came by private carriage. Sarah, m'dear, the veritable crème de la crème of the polite world is here now in our theater! Lured by the reputation of our Tidswell! Our fortunes are made! Mark my words, m'dear, after tonight's performance, word of your brother's genius will spread like wildfire."

Sarah Romney refrained from comment. She hadn't the heart to prick his bubble. It would burst of its own accord far too soon. There was no aspect of the company's endeavor she was not involved with, including its finances. Like her stepfather, she knew that tonight's house would not pay their bills. Unlike him, she did not think that the presence of three temporarily displaced young men from the first ranks of society would in any way affect their dismal future.

"Heavens, child, you aren't in costume!" Mr. Romney pulled himself back from a rosy contemplation of that future to exclaim. "Mustn't hold up the curtain. Most unprofessional. Now, get along with you."

While under discussion, the three gentlemen of the ton sat side by side in the stage box—disdainful, keyed-up, detached, as befit their various personalities. Their senses were assailed by the sights and sounds and smells of a provincial theater. Especially the smells: tallow, sawdust, orange peel, and the patrons of the pit. Mr. Langford pulled a lacy handkerchief from his sleeve and applied its perfume delicately to his nose. "Do you realize we've still some five hours of this to endure?"

"Want to go now? I won't stop you." The Honorable Randolph Milbanke received a cool stare in reply.

For probably the first time in their aristocratic lives, the three cousins had arrived for a performance before curtain time. Back at the inn where they'd engaged rooms for the night, they had discussed the matter at some length. The problem was the playbill. After arriving in Portsmouth expecting an ensemble performance by the Romney Company, they had been taken aback to discover that they'd stumbled instead upon a solo benefit by Master Tidswell. They were, however, somewhat heartened to read in fine print at the bottom of the advertisement that this performance was to be "assisted by Miss Romney." The rub was that the gentlemen had no idea of the scope of this assistance. So when Lord Graymarsh had advocated waiting until seven—or possibly even eight—to arrive at the theater, his younger brother had pointed out, "Won't do. She could assist in the first half hour and never be seen on stage again." And when Mr. Langford had advocated that they "stay in the inn, have the landlord mix a bowl of punch, and deal the cards till the whole thing's over and we can go backstage with a bouquet apiece," it was again Randolph who had immediately seen the flaw in this course of action. "Too risky. If the girl's a fright, it's better to find it out from the audience beforehand. Bad form to drop our flowers and bolt the minute she's presented." For once, the counsel of youth had won out over older, wiser heads.

The company manager's views on a prompt curtain had proved to be a theory, not a fact. Miss Romney, however, was not the cause of the delay. Though not due onstage for ages, she was ready at curtain time, waiting in the wings to prompt. Master Tidswell was the problem. First, he had to race outside to the alley to throw up. Next, he flatly refused to go onstage. Finally his distraught father personally dragged him onto the boards, meanwhile hissing to a stagehand to raise the curtain before the Prodigy could bolt. Unfortunately, the manager had no talent for invisibility. He was caught beating a fast retreat and was awarded catcalls and loud guffaws from the pit "groundlings."

Master Tidswell looked around him for an escape. There was none. His sister blocked the stage-right exit. His father beamed encouragement from the left. He considered leaping over the orchestra pit, then abandoned the idea as impractical. There was no help for him. He closed his glassy green eyes, drew a deep breath, and launched into his song.

Except to his father's fond and tone-deaf ears, Master Tidswell's voice had never been more than mediocre. Now the threat of puberty had given its soprano a growing tendency to crack. Fortunately, the worst of these occurrences were drowned out by the scraping of three fiddles that served as the orchestra. Still, it was hard to say which was more relieved, audience or performer, when the aria finally scraped and cracked its way to a conclusion. Thereupon the Prodigy opened his eyes, unclasped his hands, which had been held in piteous supplication, assumed a noble stance quite at variance with his strawlike hair and freckles, adjusted the flowing cape he wore, and, as evidence of his versatility, began a recitation. "*The Merchant of Venice*, by William Shakespeare," he announced.

"Good God!" After fifteen minutes of the bard, Mr. Langford's whisper from the stage box had a carrying power that the leading tragedian of the Romney Company had cause to envy. "Is he going to do the whole bedamned five acts?"

"Probably." His younger cousin joined in the titters that were coming from the pit. "It's the sort of thing these infant prodigies get up to."

Mr. Langford's ensuing groan distracted Sarah from the prompt book she was holding. She raised her eyes from the printed page, peered around the flat that concealed her in the wings and, for the first time, perused the occupants of the stage box.

For once her stepfather had not exaggerated. The three gentlemen were undoubtedly members of the quality. The fair-haired one, peering at her brother through his quizzing glass as if at some curious specimen of bug, was both the most handsome and the most disdainful-looking man she'd ever seen. The younger one beside him, his shirt points endangering his ears and his hand clapped hard against his mouth, was trying not to laugh aloud as the Prodigy's voice changed alarmingly halfway through the "quality of mercy" speech. Sarah appreciated the effort on his part. He looked quite nice. The third man, though not as handsome as the first and dressed more soberly than the second, somehow managed to appear of more consequence than either. Instead of looking amused or disgusted by the struggling performance, he seemed merely bored. No, Sarah amended her impression, *bored* was not the word. He looked detached. As though through an act of will he had removed himself from the tedium of his surroundings. Sarah found his attitude far more offensive than that of the other two.

So absorbed had she become in her observations that she had forgotten what was happening on stage. Only gradually did she become aware that something was amiss. And then she noticed the silence. Dread, ominous silence. Suddenly, it was punctuated by a snicker—then two, then several—from out front. Sarah jerked her attention away from the tonnish gentlemen and back onto the stage.

Master Tidswell had gone dry. He stood mutely, blinking up at the enormous chandelier suspended above the pit for inspiration. No help came from the crystal pendants. The dripping candles held no clue. Nor did his sister's frantic promptings from the wings ring a mental bell. Finally, after growing hoarse in the failed attempt to jog her brother's memory, Sarah accepted the fact that Shakespeare's jig was well and truly up. Fencing was to be the next display of the Prodigy's versatility. She threw down the prompt book, snatched up two swords, and rushed onstage to rescue Master Tidswell by launching him, a full half hour ahead of schedule, into phase three of his "bespeak" performance.

"Oh, my God!" This time Mr. Langford's exclamation was far more heartfelt, though, generally, not as audible. It did, however, carry down to the stage, where Miss Romney offered Master Tidswell a sword hilt with a snarling "En garde!" She heard, and had no doubt that it was meant for her.

As the duel began, the occupants of the stage box watched with horror. The Infant Prodigy was supposed to be the center of attention. The three men hardly saw him. Their eyes were riveted upon Miss Romney.

What they saw was a slight, graceful female form wearing a loosely flowing cambric shirt tucked into black satin knee smalls. A red sash was tied around her waist. It was obscure just what she was supposed to represent, a circumstance that bothered some members of the audience. "Is that the merchant of Venice?" a voice asked loudly. "No, it's a pirate," came the reply. But the men in the stage box were not concerned with pinning down the cast of characters. They had a far more pressing matter on their minds. Randolph at last voiced it. "She does look like Uncle Petherbridge," he croaked.

And indeed she did—at least in one overriding, appalling aspect. She was afflicted with his lordship's very prominent, very bulbous nose.

There was no need to call attention to that deformity. Randolph moved on to lesser things. "Don't think I've ever seen hair quite that carroty," he whispered hollowly. It *was* unlikely. For Miss Romney's crowning glory, while not quite the disaster of her proboscis, still left a great deal to be desired. "Don't think Petherbridge can take the blame for that."

"Her mother, then," Mr. Langford groaned. "And to

think our uncle said she was a 'prime 'un.' Should have known better, though, than to trust his judgment. After all, he picked out our horror of an aunt."

Lord Graymarsh's mesmerized gaze followed the duelists. Sarah had attacked the Prodigy with snarling fury but was now being beaten back into a corner amid the frenzied clash of swords. For fencing was the only part of his repertoire that Master Tidswell relished. "Take that, you villain!" he shouted. Sarah barely managed to sidestep his lunge.

Suddenly Graymarsh's shoulders began to shake. He collapsed back into his chair, weak with silent laughter, while the other two glared at him. "At least she's got good legs," he choked out.

"It ain't funny," his brother spat out.

"I heartily concur," their cousin agreed. "It's all very well for you to laugh"—Gerard's voice was bitter—"but the future for one of us is now making a spectacle—no, forgive me; I should not shift the blame. God or our uncle made the poor girl a spectacle. She is merely making a complete cake of herself."

The onstage battle raged furiously. As the Prodigy threw himself wholeheartedly into the fray, the bored audience came alive. This was, indeed, more like it. They cheered the thrusts of the young hero in the flowing cloak and booed the villain's parries. Such unaccustomed accolades went straight to Master Tidswell's head. He began to milk his part. When the trapped pirate—or whatever—managed to slip underneath his sword blade and began to back cravenly toward center stage, the spot chosen for the skirmish that would do him in, the hero could not resist the urge to play his audience. "Varlet! Poltroon!" he shouted, holding his sword aloft. "You'll not escape the taste of my cold steel so easily!" To underscore this point, he flourished his weapon in a furious arc that sliced off one of the candles from a sconce above his head. Neither he nor the enthralled audience was aware of its slithering descent down through the back folds of his cloak. Nor did his adversary realize what had happened until a tongue of flame licked above the hero's shoulder as he lunged at her. Sarah's scream owed nothing to dramatic art. She leaped forward to go to her brother's aid. He beat her back with a furious onslaught. The roar of the audience, now aware of the fire onstage, drowned out her voice as she shouted, "You're on fire, Tids!" His assailant's horrified expression and the audience's frenzy only served to heighten Tidswell's performance. His sword waved wildly as his sister dived once more to save him. It caught her broadside and knocked her flat. But even as she fell, she saw that help was on the way.

Like his cousin and his brother, the sixth Baron of Graymarsh had had his attention so fastened on the pirate—or whatever—that he was almost as slow as the onstage hero to realize that actor's plight. But in the instant he first saw the flames, he leaped from the box. He landed on the stage, dived underneath the flailing sword blade, and tackled Master Tidswell by the knees at the precise moment the Prodigy finally realized he was on fire. The boy's screams now outdid those from pit and gallery as the audience, far too aware of the hazards of fire to await the outcome, began to run and push and shove toward the various exits. Graymarsh rolled the panicked boy over and over while furiously slapping at the flames. At the same time, Sarah went racing toward the wing, where a water bucket was kept for such emergencies. Gray had just succeeded in getting the smoldering cloak off the hysterical Prodigy when Miss Romney charged back onstage with the dripping pail and dashed its contents at her brother. Her aim was off. The water missed its proper target. It caught his lordship full in the face. "Bloody hell!" he sputtered.

The stage was crowded now. Always the consummate professional, Mr. Romney had waved the curtain down as he and the rest of the company came rushing onstage, followed by the two remaining gentlemen from the box. The manager was now enfolding his sobbing son in his arms while assuring the young thespian that except for some singed hair he had escaped, miraculously, unscorched.

The same could not be said for Graymarsh. He felt the pain in his palms even as he wiped the streaming water from his face and gazed into the bluest pair of eyes he had ever seen. And the most expressive. They suffered with remorse for the drenching she had given him. As his lordship finished mopping himself with a snowy handkerchief and turned his attention to the damage done to his hands, he felt a twinge of sadness for nature's caprice. How ironic to put those lovely eyes and that hideous nose together in one face.

The pirate—or whatever—was now taking his hands tenderly in her own. The eyes in question filled with tears as she looked at his palms. "Oh, you are burned. I feared so. I don't know how I can ever begin to thank you—" She choked.

Sarah's quandary proved academic. She never even got the chance to try. She was now upstaged by an effusive rush of gratitude from her stepfather that left Lord Graymarsh embarrassed and impatient to be gone. He kept trying to rise from his kneeling position to his feet. The attempt was thwarted by a large presence looming over him, blubbering out gratitude for his son's miraculous salvation. "If it had not been for your heroic action, sir"—the tears streamed down Mr. Romney's face—"the world of the theater, I fear, would have lost its fastest-rising star."

"Indeed? Anyone we know?" Mr. Gerard Langford, who stood above the tableau, looked puzzled.

"I am, of course, referring to my son, Master Tidswell Romney"—the company manager was shocked that such a swell should prove to be slow-witted—"whose fame, thanks to the heroic action of this gentleman, will in time eclipse the reputations of the great Garrick and the mighty Kean."

Mr. Langford slowly turned and raised his quizzing glass toward the sobbing Prodigy, who was now being comforted by various female members of the company, as if to ascertain if there was perhaps something in the young actor's mien that he had missed. From his expression, it might have been concluded that there was not.

Lord Graymarsh, meanwhile, kept trying to extricate himself from Mr. Romney and out of a situation that was becoming more and more distasteful to him. But a new obstacle to this action appeared. As he tried once more to rise, a pair of hands grasped his shoulders and pushed him firmly down into a sitting position on the stage.

"What the devil—" He glared up into his brother's face.

"Here comes Miss Romney." Randolph spoke out of the corner of his mouth. "Don't forget why we're here."

"Don't be daft. Surely you can't still—" Gray began angrily.

"Of course he can," Gerard, his young cousin's unexpected ally, murmured in his lordship's ear. "Silly, don't you think, to have put up with that ghastly performance and then leave just as we're smoking out the quarry." He dabbed his handkerchief to his nose as the acrid smell of charred wool heightened the aptness of his phraseology.

Miss Romney was indeed returning from some mysterious errand that had taken her offstage. She quickly extracted Graymarsh from Mr. Romney's groveling gratitude by the simple expedient of pointing out that the Prodigy stood in need of his father's company.

But again Lord Graymarsh was foiled in an attempt to rise. Miss Romney knelt before him and took one hand gently in her own. The luminous eyes looked with pity at his palms, now completely blistered. "Oh, dear," she said, moaning.

"It looks worse than it is." For some reason, Gray felt

a need to relieve her of distress. "The burns are superficial, I believe."

"I feel so responsible," she murmured. "I should have gotten to Tidswell right away myself."

"You certainly tried." His lordship unexpectedly broke into a grin at the memory of her efforts. Sarah, who had thought him more distinguished than good-looking, suddenly revised her opinion. "I don't think Wellington's army could have broken through your brother's guard. Has Master Romney ever considered a military career?"

"Instead of acting?" The young woman was quick, Gray noted. "Unfortunately, I think not." She had released his hand and was opening a small, round box. "This salve should take most of the sting away." She dipped her fingers into the ointment and began to spread it tenderly on the burns. The mixture did seem to have healing properties. Or perhaps there was something in her gentle manner that his lordship hadn't experienced since his nursery days. At any rate, the stinging palms were soothed as the baron looked into the lovely eyes while tactfully managing to keep his gaze from straying to her nose.

His brother, towering above them, stagily cleared his throat. "Oh, I say. I do think we should introduce ourselves, Miss Romney. The gentleman whose hand you're holding is my brother, Lord Graymarsh. This is our cousin, Mr. Langford, and I'm Randolph Milbanke. Let me just say—though I must admit it seems dashed out of place now, what with all that's happened—how much I was admiring the, er, performance . . ." The prevarication died on his lips as the clear blue gaze seemed to look right through him. "I daresay," he stammered on, "I've never seen anything quite like it in my life. Have you, Gerry?" He turned in desperation to his cousin.

"Never," the other offered dryly, and earned himself an equally searching look. He half bowed in her direction.

"Charmed to make your acquaintance, Miss Romney." He might have been in some fashionable drawing room.

"Thank you, sir," she answered coolly, wiping a wisp of hair off her forehead with her wrist. The awkward gesture, made in deference to the ointment on her fingers, had an unsettling effect on Mr. Langford. He reemployed his quizzing glass. "I say, Miss Romney, forgive my mentioning it, but your hair seems somehow to have slipped its moorings. A wig, perhaps?" he added hopefully.

"Oh, my goodness!" For the first time, Sarah became aware of her appearance. With a complete disregard now for the effect of burn salve upon false hair, she snatched off the wild red wig that the company manager had decided would make her appearance more villainous. The three relatives stared with fascination at the tightly coiled, cloth-banded locks that were now exposed. Under the stage lighting, her own hair glowed a rich, dark brown. A soft sigh of relief escaped from the Honorable Randolph Milbanke.

Mr. Langford, on the other hand, was still studiously employing his quizzing glass—in the direction of Miss Romney's nose. His eye was as out-of-proportion magnified as that enlarged feature when he asked, "Er, do I dare hope, Miss Romney—frightful gaffe, of course, if I'm proved wrong—that your hair is not your only affectation?"

"Oh, my heavens!" Miss Romney clapped her hands in horror on her forgotten nose. It, too, had been the manager's idea. "Can't have the audience preferring you to the Prodigy," he'd chided when she'd objected. She was now pulling at the false proboscis. And if the residue of putty left clinging to her own quite small and classic feature might have seemed untidy at another time, to the fascinated gentlemen who were staring at her, it mattered not a whit. What had emerged from underneath the stage disguise was a young woman who, though red of face and flustered from being ogled by the three most distinguished gentlemen she had ever met, could most decidedly be termed personable and, most probably, when proper attention to her appearance had been paid, could even be classified as pretty.

An hour later, back at the Royal Hart and settled in their bespoken parlor around a steaming bowl of punch, the gentlemen in question pursued that very point. "I say, she's a beauty," Randolph opined.

"Nonsense," Mr. Langford drawled. "She's merely presentable, that's all. You've let yourself be carried away by the transformation. I collect that any time a frog suddenly turns into a prince, he's automatically pronounced handsome by contrast. Don't you agree, Gray?"

The object of the query was gazing absentmindedly into the depths of his punch cup but looked up when he heard his name. "I beg your pardon. I'm afraid I wasn't listening."

"My God, you can't be smitten!" His brother looked appalled. "Don't tell me you got more than your hands burned back there onstage, that your heart was singed as well!"

"What a perfectly ghastly play on words." The aesthetic Mr. Langford looked more pained than his cousin did with his blistered hands.

"Well, even if it ain't quite the way Lord Byron might put it, you do see what I mean. When a cove meets an heiress and then stops attending to conversations, well, what's another cove to think?"

"He could think," his brother said, "that the other fellow found the conversation boring and was trying to think how best to repair his damaged balloon."

"Fustian, though speaking of your balloon—" Randolph began, but Gerard refused to allow the talk to be diverted.

"We were discussing Miss Romney's physical attributes, Gray," he interrupted. "Randolph thinks her a nonpareil. I find her merely passable. What do you say?"

"Oh, I think you're right, Gerry. Ordinary. Except"—

he paused thoughtfully for a moment—"except for her eyes. They are extraordinary."

"Didn't I tell you!" Randolph pronounced. "I knew he wasn't indifferent. Balloons, indeed! And," he added glumly, "I guess you know, Cousin, he's already stolen a march on us. As though it ain't bad enough that he's the one with the fortune that Miss Romney's bound to favor, anyhow. Well, now the poor, deluded female thinks he's a hero. Gerry, did you see how she looked at him with those 'extraordinary' eyes? Damme, why couldn't I have noticed that that Shakespeare spouter had caught on fire? Or for that matter, I'd sooner it had been you, Gerry, who went leaping out of the stage box to the rescue."

"What an odd idea." His cousin's eyebrows rose. "As a matter of fact, I did see that the aging prodigy was on fire. But such an exertion on my part would never have occurred."

"You mean you saw—and just sat there? You're bamming me." While Randolph did not hold his cousin's character in high esteem, he was finding this revelation a bit much. "You ain't serious. Couldn't be."

"Why couldn't I?" The other paused to sip his punch. "Oh, I suppose if I had been the only person for miles around when the brat decided to turn himself into a torch, I'd have attempted to extinguish him. Though only after extracting a solemn oath that he'd never inflict a recitation of *The Merchant of Venice* on any hapless audience again. But with a whole company of theater types there in the wings having, I presume, little better to do than to snuff out one of their own— Well, really, old boy"—he turned with disapproval toward Lord Graymarsh—"I found your conduct in rather questionable taste."

"That's as may be"—Randolph kept the floor while his lordship merely smiled enigmatically—"but a pair of blistered palms may be a small price to pay for Uncle Petherbridge's fortune. And I tell you again, Gerry, he's stolen a march on us. It ain't easy to compete for a girl against a man who's just saved her little brother's life. And who has twelve thousand pounds a year to boot."

"Ah, yes, discouraging on the surface." Mr. Langford yawned. "But think of Aesop and take heart."

"Why on earth should I do a rum thing like that? Who's Aesop?"

"I collect our cousin's referring to the tale of the hare and the tortoise," Gray said. "The race isn't always to the swift, eh, Coz?" Gerard saluted Gray's erudition with his punch cup, and his lordship turned back to his little brother. "Well, he's right, you know. At least he is if I'm the hare. For I must confess that now that I've satisfied my curiosity and seen Uncle Petherbridge's by-blow, the contest fails to rouse my sporting blood. Bores me, in fact. So I'm here and now withdrawing from the pack. Abdicating. Leaving the field. You may rest assured, gentlemen, that I no longer have the slightest interest in winning the hand of the fair—or the commonplace—Miss Sarah Romney."

Chapter Three

*About half of the previous night's patrons were gath*ered in front of the Portsmouth Theatre when a curricle drawn by a handsome pair of grays drew to a stop. Randolph Milbanke turned the reins over to his tiger and climbed down to join the group gathered around the box office. A crudely printed notice announced: Theater closed indefinitely due to fire.

Randolph had stolen a march on his rivals, who were still sleeping in the inn, and had set off in pursuit of the unaware heiress. Now it would seem that he might just as well have stayed in bed himself.

"Fire, me eye!" A stoutish crone who, from her aroma, must have been an occupant of the pit snorted with indignation. "The only thing what got burned in there was us. If you ask me, they've just used fire as an excuse to split with our sixpences in their pockets.'' The rest of the rabble seemed to agree with her. Delegations of them were pounding on the various doors, shouting for the manager, and demanding their money back.

Finally, a small, rat-faced man opened the pit entrance just wide enough to be more inside than out and shouted, ''Go away! Nobody here but me, and I'm naught but the caretaker! The Romney Company's left town!'' After this announcement, he quickly oozed out of the crack and slammed the door, being steeped enough in dramatic lore to know that far too often it was the messenger with bad news who innocently suffered.

The crowd hung around a bit longer to grumble about actors, thieves, and swindlers and to vent their spleen by tossing a few souvenirs left by passing horses at the theater doorways. Randolph waited patiently until they'd all dispersed and then strolled around the building. He rapped sharply on the stage door with his walking cane and called out in his most authoritative, aristocratic tone, ''Oh, I say, you in there! Caretaker! Open up!'' After a few more poundings and, essentially, repetitions of the same command, he was rewarded by the stage door cracking open a tiny bit. ''Nobody here but me,'' Rat Face said grudgingly.

''I already know that. What I now need to find out is how I can locate the Romneys.'' Randolph clinked some coins together in his hand.

The door opened a bit wider. ''All I know is they closed down on account of the fire. Maybe they've gone on to Brighton,'' Rat Face added in a flash of inspiration. His eyes widened, though, as Randolph opened his hand. As the caretaker weighed the sixpence he'd been given to keep the whereabouts of the Romneys a secret against the young swell's silver, he found the former sadly wanting. ''There's more blunt there in your fist,'' he blurted, ''than you ever laid out for the ticket price.''

"I'm not wanting my money back," Randolph explained patiently. "I just need to find Miss Romney."

"Oh, well now, that's something else again, I'd say." Rat Face broke into a lascivious grin that displayed his blackened teeth. "Well now, it wouldn't be splittin' to help a gentry cove like you track down a bit o' muslin, now would it?"

Though inclined to deliver a facer along with the six shillings he paid for the Romneys' direction, Randolph contented himself with wiping his fingers clean from their contact with filthy, grasping hands. After all, the evil-minded caretaker wasn't as far off the mark in his assumptions as the gentleman might have wished.

The boardinghouse was quiet when a slatternly-looking landlady admitted him. Hers was a theatrical residence, she informed Randolph, where the paying guests normally slept late, but he'd find Mr. Romney already at his breakfast. She thereupon ushered him into a small back room where the company manager sat at a table, clad in a well-worn but scarlet-brave dressing gown, consuming toast and sweetbreads. There was more dismay than pleasure on his face when he looked up and spied his caller.

"I've come to inquire about Master Tidswell's health," the young man was inspired to reply to his reluctant host's choked greeting, and as a reward he saw the broad countenance first awash with relief, then wreathed in smiles.

"How kind! How uncommonly thoughtful!" Mr. Romney kept repeating as he insisted that the other man join him at the table. Randolph was more than happy to comply. He had left the inn too hurriedly to partake of breakfast and now realized that he was ravenous. He gratefully accepted the cup of tea his host provided and helped himself liberally from a mound of light wigs, while nodding sympathetically as Mr. Romney poured out a sad tale of the havoc that had been wrought upon the Prodigy's nervous system by his ordeal the night before. "The artistic temperament is a delicate thing." The manager sighed. "Though my son emerged practically unscathed, thanks to the heroic actions of your brother, sir"—the large man's eyes misted with gratitude—"I fear that the fire has seared his soul and it will take some healing time before his muse returns. In short, sir," he finished more prosaically, "the Prodigy refuses to go back onstage."

"Tsk! Tsk!" Randolph hoped that his clucking noises disguised his lack of true sympathy for a state of affairs he considered to be a blessing.

"It is a tragedy." The other man seemed to find no hollow ring in his guest's condolences. "But my consolation is that it can only be a temporary aberration. A talent like my Tidswell's cannot remain the victim of vile circumstance for long. Er, by the by"—he abruptly changed the subject—"you did say you came from the theater, did you not? Was there, er, anyone else there?"

Randolph reluctantly relayed the information that a large proportion of the previous night's patrons had turned up hoping to get their money back.

"Dear me. Dear me. I was afraid of that. And you, sir?" the manager forced himself to ask.

"No, no, of course not," Randolph assured him. "I felt more than recompensed by the first part of the performance. Wouldn't dream of profiting from your near tragedy."

It was not stage technique, Randolph concluded, that caused the manager's eyes to brim with tears at the slightest pretext. Mr. Romney was a very sentimental man. "Thank you, sir, for articulating so well my very own feelings," he choked out. "I, too, felt that the audience had, for the merest pittance, been allowed a cultural feast. And even though the feast had to be shortened, alas, by several courses, I cannot believe that so many were so crass as to ask for refunds. Well, well—in time, when our Prodigy attains the dramatic stature that fate has in store for him, those oafs will thank me for not allowing them the humiliation of being reimbursed for a foreshortened Tidswell Romney performance. In the meantime, I can only thank you for displaying in these trying times the sensitivity of a gentleman."

While Randolph basked in so much approval, the time seemed ripe to inquire after Miss Romney's health. And after being assured that the young actress had survived the previous night's ordeal like a veteran trouper, it seemed an even better notion to ask if he might see her.

But no sooner had the request left Randolph's lips than a subtle change came over the company manager. Though Mr. Romney continued to smile affably, Randolph did not miss the hint of suspicion lurking in his eyes. "Alas, my daughter's frayed nerves require rest and solitude. I'm sure you understand." And there was something in Mr. Romney's tone that made Mr. Milbanke think twice about pointing out the discrepancy between the trouper image of Miss Romney and this latest version of her mental state.

Randolph Milbanke's instincts did not play him false. Though overprone to toadeat the quality, Mr. Romney drew the line where his daughter's well-being was concerned. And though inclined to give reality a wide berth in the main, he allowed himself no such latitude regarding the motives of gentlemen in pursuit of actresses. Even this fresh-faced stripling was not likely to be exempt from temptations of the flesh. So without putting his position crassly into words, Mr. Romney made it quite clear to the slightly red-faced young gentleman that Miss Romney never socialized with her audience. "It destroys illusion," he explained. "Aesthetic distance must be maintained, you see." He smiled apologetically.

Foiled in his pursuit of the Petherbridge fortune for the day, Randolph was anxious to know where the Romney Company would go from there. This wasn't easy to pin down. There was quite a lot said about "pausing at artistic crossroads'' and ''weighing the various possibilities.'' An ''almost certain booking'' seemed anticipated, but only ''if this or that takes place.'' A lot more bluster followed in a similarly optimistic vein. But when the young gentleman finally took his cordial leave of the actor-manager, he was left with the distinct impression that the Romney Company was well up the River Tick and hadn't the slightest notion what it would do next.

It was a very thoughtful Randolph Milbanke who drove the ten miles to Pether Hall. How he was to be expected to pursue a young female who was guarded at home by a suspicious father and taken out of the public domain by the collapse of her career was more than he could fathom. Even keeping track of Miss Romney's whereabouts could prove impossible. Adolphus Romney's rambling references to Bath and Bournemouth had been duly noted and filed in memory. But then, when the sanguine manager had begun to talk of London, Randolph realized that all of his plans were just so much moonshine. The Romney Company had been delivered a knockout blow and would likely remain down for the full count.

Randolph's only comfort was that if he was stymied in his pursuit of his uncle's heiress, his rival—or rivals, for he was not fully convinced of his brother's withdrawal from the chase—was completely in the dark. The coins he'd given the theater caretaker had persuaded that worthy to lock up his doors and visit the nearest tavern. Randolph didn't doubt that he'd be there for the day, and anyone else looking for the Romneys would find only an empty theater.

As for himself, he'd no intention of being questioned about his morning's activities, hence his decision to head for his great-uncle's house. At least he'd be in the vicinity of Portsmouth and could check on the Romneys' movements while, he hoped, his two rivals headed back to London. Besides, it might be helpful to report the current state of affairs to Lord Petherbridge. After all, it occurred to the nephew, the old rake had had experience in pursuing actresses and might be persuaded to part with some helpful advice.

But Randolph was doomed to disappointment on that score. When he arrived at the hall, Lord Petherbridge was sequestered with his bailiff and likely to remain so for some time. Lady Petherbridge, however, the butler informed him, was in her chamber. Randolph suppressed a sigh and went in search of his prosy relative.

"Oh, it's you." Lady Petherbridge looked up from her cluttered writing table with a preoccupied gaze. "Good. You can help me."

Randolph stared back at his elderly relative with some astonishment. He was not accustomed to her ladyship being pleased to see him. Well, not *pleased* precisely, he amended. Her expression was more of the "any old port in a storm" variety.

Indecision did not become Lady Petherbridge. The frilled cap that almost obscured the iron-gray hair, and whose ruffled fasteners shored up several chins, outlined a face accustomed to command. The snapping eyes below a beetled brow and above a nose fit to grace a Caesar could, under normal circumstances, pale a butler and reduce a housemaid to tears with a single stare. But now the face appeared as close to bemusement as such an august assortment of features could permit. "Sit down, Randolph." Her ladyship waved imperiously at a chair. "I need your advice."

It took all her nephew's self-control to keep his chin from dropping. Indeed, a summons from His Majesty to discuss affairs of state would have been no more astounding. Randolph obediently pulled the chair closer to the table, collapsed in it, and looked at his aunt warily.

"It's your uncle," she said abruptly. "I'm worried about him. Do you realize he's been on his deathbed three times in the last six months?"

"That often? Well, no, er, yes. But I, uh, don't think, actually—"

His aunt waved him to silence. "Oh, I know Petherbridge ain't really dying. That's just the point. He's turned morbid. And it ain't like him to be blue-deviled. So it's up to us to cheer him up."

"Us? Well, I, er—"

Lady Petherbridge rolled once more over the interruption. "I hold myself responsible." To her nephew's astonishment—and horror—he saw tears begin to form in her ladyship's eyes. "I fear that my more serious-minded nature has put your uncle under a great strain. He was used, you know, before he met and married me, to live a frivolous, pleasure-filled existence. And while I cannot but condemn a life given over totally to the pursuit of pleasure when there are so many worthy causes crying for attention, still I can see that for a person of your uncle's temperament such a radical change from the frivolous to the significant could in time exact a toll. And in your uncle's case I believe this excess of morbidity is the direct result of this change in his mode of living. And since I value your uncle's well-being even more than the demands of principle, I have decided to take drastic measures." She paused dramatically while Randolph gazed at her, wide-eyed. "I shall give a house party!"

Her voice rang out with martyred resolution. Her face glowed like Joan of Arc's. "That's why I'm glad to see you, Randolph," she added in more normal tones. "I need your suggestions on how to entertain my guests."

If thereupon Randolph stared at her, transfixed, it was not, as Lady Petherbridge suspected, that his faculties had stalled. In point of fact, his mind was racing at an accelerated speed that he found frightening. It struck him that in just such a sudden burst of frenzied inspiration might the "Hallelujah Chorus" have occurred to Handel. None of this, however, conveyed itself upon his vacant countenance. Indeed, Lady Petherbridge was moved to snap her fingers in his face.

"Don't gawk, boy. I'm making a perfectly reasonable request of you. You go to parties, don't you? Of course you do. And while you ain't an arbiter of fashion as Gerard is, you must surely know how the frivolous amuse themselves. I certainly do not. The only houses I ever went to were the ones where the talk was serious."

Randolph repressed a shudder. There was a time, he recalled, when his aunt had been affiliated with the Society for the Suppression of Vice, whose members warred on Sabbath breakers, licentious books, dram shops, county fairs, and all other distractions of the devil. Her marriage had modified her zeal, however. Her causes now took a more positive turn.

"Speak up, Randolph." She was looking at him impatiently. "You must surely have some suggestion for entertaining our houseguests."

Randolph beamed. His hour had come. "As a matter of fact, I have. Theatricals."

"Theatricals!" Her ladyship thundered like a major prophet as her black eyes snapped their disapproval. And only then did her great-nephew recall that private theatricals were among the vices that the Society for the Suppression of had targeted. Even so, Randolph held his ground.

"Just the ticket for Uncle," he said firmly, although he dropped his eyes before the gimlet gaze. "Nothing like a play to take a chap right out of himself. I refer, of course, to the highest type of uplifting drama that points up a moral principle," he threw in with a cunning Machiavelli could have admired. "I mean the sort of thing those old Greek coves seemed to think could purge the soul." He risked a look at his aunt. Her expression had transposed from outraged to thoughtful. "Hmmm," she said.

Rightly interpreting the syllable for indecision, Randolph pressed on. "It's done, you know, in the very best houses.

Uncle would like it above all things. And there's a bang-up theater in the hall."

"That's true, but—"

Under normal circumstances, Randolph would never have dared to interrupt his august aunt. But there was nothing normal about this situation. Handel's misplaced muse still whispered in his ear. "And you wouldn't have to concern yourself at all. The custom is to invite some professional actress to take—"

"Randolph!" Lady Petherbridge trumpeted. "Have you gone mad?"

"W-why, no, ma'am." He gulped.

"Then I can only assume that you're indulging in some tasteless joke. But I assure you, I am not amused."

"It ain't a joke, ma'am." The thought of the fortune at stake gave the young man courage. "It's quite the thing. To bring in somebody who knows what's what to pull everything together. And maybe to play the lead while the houseguests do the other parts. But mainly to direct the thing."

Any charity Lady Petherbridge had momentarily felt for her nephew was fading fast. The frosty look she bent upon him raised gooseflesh despite the sun-drenched room. "I cannot believe, sir, that you are seriously suggesting that I extend the hospitality of Pether Hall to a creature of that ilk! An actress! As my houseguest! Never!"

"But I ain't suggesting *that* sort of actress. Wouldn't dream of it. Had in mind someone more like the Kembles—a terribly respectable theatrical family, you know. Received in the best houses. Friends of Lord and Lady Egerton. Spotless reputations."

Her ladyship wavered. "Well, yes, the Kembles. But you must admit, Randolph, they are the exception and not the rule in what is generally a degenerate profession."

"All the more reason, don't you think, to lend a helping hand to actors trying to lead decent lives. There's this one theatrical family in particular—not well known like the Kembles, but they've managed to uphold high moral standards in their profession, too. But now they're down on their luck, due to an accident to their child prodigy."

"To their what?"

"Child prodigy. That's an odd sort of youngster who recites Shakespeare by the bucketful and gets up to all sorts of other queer starts that children ain't usually up to doing."

"I know what a prodigy is, Randolph," his aunt said witheringly. "And I must say I abhor the very idea of a mere child being exploited."

"Well, I'm with you there, ma'am." Randolph shuddered at the memory of *The Merchant of Venice*.

"It should be stopped."

"Well, in this particular case it has been," Randolph began, but the light of zeal was beginning to glow in his aunt's eyes, and she did not hear him.

"This is a *respectable* theatrical family, you say?"

"Oh, yes, indeed." Randolph began to describe the Romneys in glowing and fictitious terms that included Sunday school for the Prodigy and baskets of theatrical oranges distributed to the needy by Miss Romney. "But now they've been forced to close their engagement early—and, well, they're destitute. So I thought it would be an act of charity to engage Miss Romney for the theatricals, don't you see, and save a deserving family from sinking to the level of those types you disapprove of. And at the same time, a play could give Uncle a real lift."

Lady Petherbridge was almost convinced. "You are quite certain, Randolph, of the young woman's character?"

"The very soul of respectability, I assure you." There was a sincerity in his tone that nipped the seeds of suspicion in his aunt's mind as to his motives before they could begin to sprout. "And she looks and talks like a lady." He pressed his advantage. "Wouldn't put off your other guests. Uncle would—"

"Very well, then." Lady Petherbridge had made her snap decision and was ready to move on to other things. "I shall write to Miss Romney and engage her and her little brother."

"Her b-brother? Oh, I say, I don't really think that the Prodigy'd fit in at a house party." Randolph was appalled. "Besides, he wouldn't be up to performing just yet. Had an accident, you see."

"That, Randolph, is the point." His aunt stood dismissively, glaring down her impressive nose at her great-nephew. "He shall not perform. I intend to give the child the benefit of country air, good food, and a moral environment. I want to expose him to life away from the evil theater and plant his feet on the path of righteousness. I'm beginning to regard this house party as heaven-sent. What I had considered selfish indulgence and crass frivolity can now serve a higher purpose. I shall reclaim this child from his sordid calling."

"B-but—"

"Don't try to dissuade me from my duty, young man." His aunt thrust a sheet of paper into his hands and gestured toward the pen and inkwell on the table. "Just write down the Romneys' direction and I will do the rest. My conscience would not be easy if I ignored the plight of that hapless child. Indeed, Randolph, I see the infant prodigy as a brand that must be plucked immediately from the burning."

"Oh, no, Aunt Augusta. That ain't necessary. You see—"

"A brand to be plucked from the burning," she stated once more, emphatically.

"But I don't think you understand, ma'am." Confused by the biblical terminology, Randolph felt a need to set the record straight. "Don't know how you could have learned about the burning part, but the thing is, Gray's already done the plucking. No need to concern yourself at all."

''The Romneys' direction, Randolph.'' Lady Pether-bridge snapped her fingers.

''Yes, Aunt Augusta.'' With a sigh for a brilliant scheme gone half awry, the Honorable Randolph Milbanke seated himself, dipped the pen in ink, and began to write.

Chapter Four

The London stage was due to depart in five minutes, and the Royal Hart bustled with activity. So much so that the landlord hadn't time to assess properly the young woman inquiring after Lord Graymarsh. His first inclination as he glanced at her respectable-looking, if unfashionable, dark walking dress and listened to her modulated, cultured voice was to have the boot escort her to a private parlor, then go fetch his lordship. No sooner had the thought occurred than the boy himself staggered down the stairs lumbered by a pile of luggage bound for the metropolis. "Who'll I say's calling?" the host inquired as he settled the reckoning with the owner of the baggage.

"Miss Romney from the Portsmouth Theatre," the young woman replied, and earned a startled stare. That settled that. An actress. Didn't look the type, but facts were facts. At ten in the morning. By herself. Bold as brass. The landlord, a family man, tried to stifle a look of disapproval. Business was business, and he couldn't afford to antagonize the gentry. Having the likes of Lord Graymarsh in his inn was bound to do wonders for the reputation of the Royal Hart. That is, if he didn't set the quality's backs up by not blinking at their rakeshame ways. Funny thing, though. He'd have thought that his lordship was the least likely to . . . Well, it was none of his concern. "Upstairs, left corridor, third door on the left," he said dismissively as he counted out the traveler's change.

Sarah hadn't missed the landlord's disapproval and for the first time paused to consider that her mercy mission might be open to misinterpretation. Certainly Miss Marshall at the Marshall Academy for Young Ladies, a second-rate boarding school with pretensions of gentility, had drummed it into her pupils' heads that no proper young lady went abroad unaccompanied. As for visiting a gentleman in his rooms—well, that was so unthinkable as to have never been discussed. Miss Romney was, however, of the theater, which had a different code. And if, in her case at least, that code did not include the type of behavior that Lady Petherbridge so heartily disapproved of, still it did embrace a degree of independence. Even so, Miss Romney was prey to second thoughts as she rapped rather timidly upon the designated chamber door.

Inside, Lord Graymarsh had, for once, regretted traveling without his valet. His hands, while not seriously burned, had smarted enough during the night to make sleeping difficult. He had counteracted this by drinking a great deal more brandy than he was used to. As a result, he had a throbbing head as well as smarting palms. Shaving had been an ordeal, since the razor had been difficult to hold. The nicks on his face testified to the difficulty. The soft tapping on the door hit his head like drumbeats, causing him to flinch and to add a new notch to his chin.

"Damnation!" he swore as he dipped the corner of a towel into the washbowl and growled, "Come in."

Sarah stepped inside and then felt her face flame red. His lordship, stripped to the waist, was standing in front of the washstand holding a towel to his chin, his full attention focused on the looking glass as he tried to staunch the flow of blood. Later she was to remember, in a rush of embarrassment, that if she hadn't been so stunned by the sight of broad shoulders, rippling muscles, and a thatch of dark chest hair, she could have simply backed out of the doorway and disappeared. But for some reason Lord Graymarsh in dishabille affected her wits adversely. Her widened eyes traveled down skintight pantaloons, registered muscular thighs, and came to rest with a shock on his lordship's bare feet. This homey sight jarred her back to reality once again, and she was just about to do her disappearing act when Gray glanced her way and the opportunity was lost forever.

Lord Graymarsh, who had expected to see a servant, was almost as jolted as Miss Romney. But in his case surprise was quickly displaced by disappointment, a reaction that, if he'd stopped to analyze it before it quickly faded, would have surprised him.

Lord Graymarsh was well accustomed to pursuit. In fact, he had become bored by it in all its forms, whether exhibited in the coquettish glances over French silk fans at Almack's or by the more blatant sexual advances of the fashionable impures. Even so, his moment of disappointment had come from one more illusion shattered. Miss Romney of the clear blue eyes and tender concern had not struck him as a lady of easy virtue. Still, as her presence here in his room reminded him, she was, after all, a common actress. And her mother's daughter. As well as Lord Petherbridge's.

If Sarah had been quick to notice the landlord's attitude, Graymarsh's was even clearer as he looked at her with a cynical, and bloodshot, stare. "I—I came to inquire about your hands," she stammered in a rush of embarrassment that might have given Gray second thoughts if he hadn't concluded that she was acting.

"Thank you," he said dryly, hanging up the towel but not bothering to put on the dressing gown flung carelessly on a bedpost. The sight of the unmade bed, which seemed to be expanding before her eyes until it filled the entire room, made Sarah even more uncomfortable. With an effort, she wrenched her attention away from it. Lord Graymarsh looked down at his palms indifferently. "The burns are beginning to heal." He held his hands out toward her. "Would you like to take a look?" This time she did not care for his smile—or leer—at all.

Again it took an effort to remind herself that she had come on a mercy mission. "Did the salve help?" She might have been a doctor inquiring clinically about a patient's treatment.

He laughed softly. "Come see for yourself." She hadn't moved from her station by the door.

"You forgot to take the ointment with you," she continued, "and I thought you might be needing it. We've found it to be very efficacious."

" 'Efficacious'?" His gray eyes mocked her use of the high-toned word. "Oh, I'm sure it's all of that and more."

"Well, at any rate, here it is if you need it again," she said primly, preparing to set the ointment on the chest of drawers next to the door and then take her leave. She was inwardly upbraiding her foolish conduct. And wondering why this odious man had appealed to her so much the night before. It hadn't been just his physical attraction, which he seemed so well aware of, that she'd found compelling then. There'd been something else that she'd fancied she had seen in him. Sarah felt a sudden rush of disappointment that put Gray's similar reaction to shame. For after all, her experience with the opposite sex had been far more limited than his. Her disillusionment came harder.

"That ointment can't be 'efficacious' unless applied, now can it?" he said mockingly as she set it down. "Last night, you put it on for me." He found her missishness a bit absurd under the circumstances and was baiting her. Sarah realized this, resented it, and decided to settle the matter once and for all.

It was certainly out of character for her to be so unnerved by a shirtless, bootless gentleman. There was no time in the theater for such niceties as the insistence on privacy for costume changes. She'd seen many an actor in worse states of undress than this, she told herself as she snatched the box of ointment off the chest and took a determined, if unwary, step in his direction. It was her misfortune then to trip over his carelessly discarded Hessians and go sprawling into his arms.

Lord Graymarsh may have been disgusted by Miss Romney's blatant pursuit, but he was also human. When he found himself supporting a young woman who was clinging to his naked chest and whose "extraordinary" blue eyes widened with feigned shock as they met his narrowed gray ones, he did what any other red-blooded gentleman would have done. He kissed her.

And it came as no surprise that Miss Romney cooperated. The only surprise was the heady pleasure the encounter brought him, a feeling almost, but not quite, new. Indeed, the softness of the lips that met his own with unexpected sweetness and then parted in response to his awakened passion was enough to make him forget his stinging hands and throbbing head.

Sarah, on the other hand, had no basis for comparison. She was caught off guard by this new development. Indeed, so bombarded was she by a variety of strange emotions that being lifted off her feet at first appeared to be just natural cause and effect, a normal state of levitation. The contact of their kiss was, however, fortuitously broken as he deposited her upon that disconcerting bed and climbed in beside her. The momentary release brought Sarah to her senses. "What do you think you're doing, sir?" she yelped.

Gray, who had momentarily upstaged his headache with desire, felt it return full force, and all his ill humor with it. "Look, Miss Romney—Sarah, or whatever it is you're called—don't you think it's time you dropped the missish role? I'm in no mood for plays. What I'm doing is precisely what you came up here for, so let's get on with it. Now, where were we?" He reached for her again. Sarah boxed his ear and leaped off the bed.

"Oh, I say, Miss Romney, is my cousin annoying you?"

Gray groaned. Whether it was the ringing slap or the sight of his dapper cousin lounging in the doorway with his infernal quizzing glass in place that had increased the pain in his throbbing head was merely academic. "Go straight to hell, Gerry," he muttered.

"On the contrary, dear boy. I should say that it's you who are on the path to perdition. Assaulting young ladies? In Portsmouth? In midmorning? Not at all the thing, you know." The blistering look his cousin flashed his way did nothing to disturb the expression of shocked rectitude on Gerard's face.

Sarah, in the meantime, was looking around for her bonnet, which had gone missing somewhere along the line. It did nothing for her agitation to discover the demure dark-blue headgear underneath the bed. The final indignity was to go down on her knees to retrieve it under the jaundiced eye of Lord Graymarsh and the interested gaze of the Corinthian by the door.

Well aware of her flaming cheeks, she clapped on the bonnet and fastened its ribbons with a jerk that nearly choked her. The salve, too, had landed on the floor. Sarah scooped it up defiantly. Let his lordship's roaming hands heal themselves! As far as she was concerned, they deserved to smart.

It took all her actor's training to hold her head high. She made her exit without a backward glance at the half-dressed gentleman still seated on the bed watching her. But she could not avoid looking at Mr. Langford. He blocked the doorway. Sympathy was written largely upon his face. He was enjoying the scene immensely, though, Sarah was sure.

"Allow me to see you safely home, Miss Romney."

"That won't be necessary."

"Beg pardon, but I have to differ. You need a protector, obviously. This world is filled with villains just waiting to take advantage of unescorted ladies, I'm afraid." He smiled wickedly over her shoulder at his cousin. Gray's bloodshot glare of bottled-up outrage made his grin grow broader.

Sarah was too anxious to leave Graymarsh's odious presence to stand and argue. She feared she might succumb to impulse and hurl the salve at his lordship's aristocratic head. But after she'd stalked down the stairs in embarrassed, indignant silence, run the gauntlet of the landlord and his servants' curious eyes, and emerged finally into the inn yard, she turned to her companion. "Really, sir, I thank you for your consideration, but I should prefer to go on alone."

"It isn't done, you know," the other replied pleasantly, taking her arm. "You must break this habit of going unescorted. It gives the wrong impression."

She opened her mouth to protest, but the innkeeper had brought his curiosity to the door. Defeated, she turned toward home with the Corinthian in tow.

"Really, Miss Romney, I must protest the pace!" After they'd walked rapidly for several minutes, Gerard broke the silence. "My weak heart may not stand the strain."

She gave him a withering glance that took in his muscular physique. "It's my guess that in addition to being an accomplished horseman—as your kind always seems to be—you spar in Cribb's Parlour. Am I not right?'' He nodded. ''Then I do not think that this little bit of exercise will harm you. But if you're concerned, you may stop and rest. I did not desire your company, you recall.''

''Really, Miss Romney.'' He regained her arm, which she'd removed from his, and slowed her down. ''It's most unfair of you to heap my cousin's sins upon my innocent head.'' His smile was intended to disarm.

Sarah, though, had no reason to revise her first impression, that he cared not a fig for anyone but himself. She still considered him the handsomest man she'd ever seen. He looked almost as elegant in his tall beaver hat, dark spencer jacket, and biscuit-colored pantaloons as he had in black and white evening clothes. And he was obviously exerting himself to charm her. What she couldn't understand was why.

Mr. Langford, aware of her suspicion, heaved a heavy, stagey sigh. ''I really can't blame you for being out of charity with my 'kind.' I believe that was your term. My cousin's caddish behavior is enough to prejudice any sensitive young lady. Let me see if I can reconstruct what happened.''

''That won't be necessary,'' she said between stiff lips. ''What happened was quite evident.''

''Yes, but actions divorced from motives are most unsatisfactory witnesses of character. Don't you agree?'' He gave her a moment to comment, then, when she failed to do so, went on. ''You, for instance, felt compelled, out of gratitude for Lord Graymarsh's rescue of your brother and a genuine concern for the hurt he suffered, to seek out my cousin this morning with your cure-all. Your motives were pure and altruistic. Am I not right?''

Sarah refused to look at him or to acknowledge that she was listening. For in truth she had no desire to explore her motives. But Mr. Langford was forcing her to admit—only to herself, of course—that she really had wished to see

Lord Graymarsh once again. But she certainly had not wished to be kissed by him or to be . . .

Gerard continued his one-sided conversation. "But looked at from my cousin's point of view, your visit took on an entirely different connotation. You see, my dear Miss Romney, Gray's been terribly spoiled from the cradle on. You are aware that he is most sinfully wealthy, are you not?" Sarah wasn't and said as much but didn't think the Corinthian believed it for a moment. "He's never been denied anything, don't you see. And that includes the, er, favors of the fairer sex. I'm afraid, Miss Romney, that females have the regrettable habit of flinging themselves at my cousin's head."

Sarah's cheeks, which had finally cooled down, heated up again. "Fling themselves." That's exactly what she'd appeared to do, thanks to his lordship's ill-placed boots.

"And if you'll forgive me," the gentleman was saying, "your habit of going about without a maid or footman in attendance only served to reinforce my cousin's, er, regrettable misconception."

"Mr. Langford." For the first time, Miss Romney looked him full in the face. "I am well aware that Lord Graymarsh took me for a trollop." The Corinthian's eyebrows rose at such plain speaking. "And you are right. I did bring the slander upon myself. I'm afraid I tend to forget that actresses have that sort of reputation, whether deserved or not. Another characteristic of actresses is that, except for a highly successful few, they do not have maids or footmen at their beck and call. However, my mistake was not in going unaccompanied to see your cousin. It was in going to see your cousin at all." They had reached the gate that barred the path to her rooming house. She forestalled Gerard's gallantry by opening it herself. "Good day, Mr. Langford," she said firmly. "Thank you for your escort."

He cocked an eyebrow and smiled winningly. "May I not come in and recover from our canter?"

"I think you will survive it. If there's doubt, you'll find a coffeehouse one street over."

"Heartless! When may I see you again?"

"Watch for the playbills. I'm sure the Romney Company will be back in production soon."

"That was not what I meant, vixen, and you know it."

"It was what I meant, Mr. Langford," she answered coolly. "The only communication I intend to have with any member of the quality again will be from stage to audience. Good day, sir." Sarah walked swiftly up the gravel pathway and disappeared into the house without a backward glance. Mr. Langford stared at the closed door speculatively.

Chapter Five

The Honorable Randolph Milbanke had never been im- pressed by his own intellect. But now he was seriously contemplating a life in government, guiding the ship of state through troubled waters. For getting his aunt Augusta to invite Miss Romney to Pether Hall had been a diplomatic coup.

True, having the prodigy included in the invitation was a bit depressing, and finding his brother's and his cousin's names on the proposed guest list was downright dampening. But as his uncle's valet withdrew after putting the final touch to the young visitor's cravat, Randolph preened in the cheval glass at the memory of the inspired way he'd scotched his rivals. He'd subtly persuaded his unsuspecting aunt to extend invitations to Lady Scriven, the wealthy widow who was determined that Gerard Langford fill her late lord's shoes, and Miss Evelina Crome, the newest candidate for his brother's hand.

He could count on Lady Scriven to keep Gerard occupied. But Miss Crome, he realized, though a beauty without peer, would not, on her own, pose much of a threat to Gray's bachelorhood. She was fresh from the schoolroom, and shy to boot, with none of Lady Scriven's determination. But that lack caused him no concern. Randolph was well aware that the beauty's mama possessed the required resolution by the bucketful. And since there was no question of Miss Crome's being invited without Lady Emma as a chaperon, Randolph was assured of having the unwitting heiress, Miss Romney, to himself. He was humming a cheerful little tune as he left his bedchamber to go in search of whatever diversion might be found that morning at Pether Hall.

He was not alarmed when Mason announced lugubriously, "Lord Petherbridge would like a word with you in the library, sir." There was nothing unusual in the butler's mournful attitude. A simple announcement such as "Dinner is served" had a way of sounding like the trump of doom from Mason's mouth. So Randolph was still humming as he opened the library door.

The sight of his uncle's livid countenance froze the melody on his lips. "Close the door, Randolph," Lord Petherbridge commanded with hard-won control. No sooner was the heavy portal in place, however, than he exploded. He took a threatening step toward his nephew. "What the devil are you up to, you—you bedlamite!"

"I—I don't think I understand, sir." Randolph placed a shaky hand upon the doorknob, considering flight.

"*You* don't understand!" his uncle thundered. "*I* don't understand! What possessed you, lad?" Lord Petherbridge's wrath suddenly gave way before his sense of injury. To his nephew's increased horror, his chin quivered and his eyes brimmed with tears. "How could ye betray me?"

"B-betray you, sir? Oh, I say! There's bound to be some sort of mixup. I haven't betrayed you, sir. Wouldn't dream of such a thing."

Anyone else might have been struck by the young man's obvious sincerity. Not so Lord Petherbridge. The only effect it had was to swing his emotional pendulum back to wrath. "Do ye deny, sir, that you've hoaxed your aunt into inviting me by-blow to this house?"

"Oh, that." The mystery was apparently cleared up, but for some reason Randolph did not feel enlightened.

"Yes, that! Of all the shabby, underhanded, scurvy, knavish—"

Just as the uncle ran out of adjectives, the nephew's sense of injustice shored up his manhood. "Oh, I say, sir. That's coming it a bit strong!"

"Not a bit of it. It don't begin to describe what I think of your treachery."

"Treachery!" Randolph gasped. "What does treachery have to say to anything? I think that having Aunt Augusta invite Miss Romney to direct her theatricals was a capital idea, if I do say so myself. And for the life of me I can't see why you're in such a pucker over it."

Randolph regretted the words immediately. The resulting near apoplexy was indeed alarming. He was contemplating ringing the bell for Mason when his lordship recovered enough to gasp, "You actually think it's 'capital' to have Augusta find out she's playing hostess to me bastard?"

Randolph did wish his uncle would be less basic in his terminology and almost said so, but on further reflection decided to save such chiding for another day. "Of course I didn't think it would be capital for Aunt Augusta to find out that Miss Romney's your daughter. What an extraordinary notion. There's no way she'll find out. Who's going to tell her?'' His eyes were filled with injured rectitude. ''You should know that Gray won't. And even Gerry, who's rackety in some ways, wouldn't dream of doing such a shabby thing. So you must mean me. And I have to say it—in spite of all your years, and even if it means the inheritance—I resent your implications!''

Randolph's wounded attitude gave his uncle pause. The old gentleman took a deep breath before he answered. His tone was almost normal. ''It's bound to come out, though, once the girl gets here. Augusta will know at once. Never could keep anything from her.''

''That's not exactly so, sir,'' Randolph ventured, and then hurried on as his lordship bristled again. ''You've kept your secret for twenty-one or twenty-two years, and there's nothing in Miss Romney's appearance or manner to give you away.''

''You're saying the girl ain't like me at all?''

Randolph couldn't tell whether there was relief or disappointment in his uncle's attitude. But he hastened to describe Miss Romney in glowing terms and to assure his lordship that the young actress, as predicted, evidently looked like her mother. ''So nobody, not even Aunt Augusta, could possibly guess at the relationship.''

''The girl could tell 'em.''

Randolph's mouth flew open. That thought hadn't occurred to him. ''You mean she knows?''

''I've no idea. Her mother died when she was still a child. So I doubt the two of them ever sat down to chat about the thing. But mark me words, her mother's bound to have told somebody who's bound to have told the girl. Oh, you've put the cat among the pigeons for sure, lad, by asking that young woman to come and stay here.''

''But sir, you did go on and on about wanting to see your own flesh and blood under your roof.''

''That's when I'm dead and gone, you ninny. I certainly didn't intend to stir up a hornets' nest while I'm still alive.''

"There won't be a hornets' nest," his nephew replied with firm conviction. "I'll bet a monkey Miss Romney don't know a thing about the relationship, and even if she does know, it don't signify. Actress or no actress, Miss Romney's a lady. She ain't at all the type to tie her garters in public; you can rest assured of that, sir. Besides," he pointed out, "if you're serious about wanting one of us to marry her, it's a risk you'll have to take. For frankly, if she don't come here, I don't know how the deuce we'll get the chance to court her." He then went on to inform his uncle of how the stage manager kept Sarah cloistered when not performing. "And the company's folded, sir. She ain't likely to be acting anytime soon. So we can't go backstage to dangle after her."

Randolph continued to press his points and finally convinced his uncle that the visit of his illegitimate daughter, while not the most comfortable of arrangements, was necessary for the continuation of the Petherbridge line. After a dismissal that, though grumpy, was still a thousandfold more cordial than his reception, Randolph closed the library door behind him and mopped his brow. "For a cove so deuced anxious to have his own flesh and blood here at the hall, the old boy certainly kicked up a dust when I tried to help it happen," he muttered to himself. "You'd have thought he'd want to thank me. Fall on my neck in gratitude and all that sort of thing. Just goes to show. Virtue has to be its own reward." On that self-righteous note, he headed for the solace of the billiard table.

Miss Romney was only slightly less disturbed than Lord Petherbridge over the fact that she was being invited to Pether Hall. When her crested invitation arrived, she had to read the crossed message several times and then recheck the outside of the missive to see if she was really the intended recipient. For the invitation made no sense. Sarah had never heard of Lady Petherbridge and could not imagine what had possessed the noblewoman to engage her to entertain the guests asked to Pether Hall. She took the note and her puzzlement to Adolphus Romney.

" 'O my prophetic soul!' " The company manager struck an attitude. "Did I not predict that something like this would happen? Our fortunes are made!"

"I wouldn't go quite that far," Sarah said dryly. She had found the manager sitting morosely in the front parlor, gazing with glassed-over eyes through the window at the bustling street. But now he leaped from the slough of despair and became his old ebullient self again. "I'd hardly call a pound apiece for Tids and me a fortune. For a fortnight's work, it's hardly handsome."

Mr. Romney's gesture waved away such monetary consideration. No one but Sarah would have suspected he hadn't a feather left to fly with. "What payment you receive for your contribution to the success of her ladyship's house party is totally beside the point, my dear. What is important is that you and Tidswell will find yourselves at last in your proper milieu. And to think I was concerned over our closing! The Portsmouth Theatre—bah!" His sneer recalled Richard III's contempt. "We'll be able to bid farewell to the provinces after this and take our rightful place on the London stage."

Sarah was too accustomed to her stepfather's high flights to refine much on them. Instead, she kept frowning at her letter as if by staring long enough she'd unravel the mystery of it. "I still don't understand why they're asking us," she muttered.

Her stepfather looked slightly offended. "That should be self-evident, my dear. Where else would her ladyship find a juvenile of Tidswell's genius and an actress with your birth and breeding?"

"Almost anywhere," Sarah was on the verge of saying, but held her tongue.

"After all, my dear, breeding tells. You must recall that

I did explain when you were but a child, though the subject was almost too painful for me to broach, that you yourself are of the aristocracy. I do not condone your poor, dear mother's folly''—he wiped an eye rather ostentatiously—''nor do I condemn it. But I have found comfort in the fact that her earlier love was of the highest rank. There could be no question of marriage, needless to say. They were as star-crossed as Romeo and Juliet. Their tragedy was, of course, my own good fortune. Otherwise I might never have won your mother's hand.'' He wiped the other eye.

It was a story Sarah had heard several times before. The main difference in this telling was that Mr. Romney's recital was without benefit of port. And she had noticed through the years that her natural father's rank tended to increase with repetition. She would not be surprised, she was used to think, if one day her begetting was credited to the crown prince himself.

Sarah had never refined much upon the story. Illegitimacy was not uncommon in her world, and many actresses were fond of assigning noble antecedents to their nameless offspring. The great Edmund Kean was a case in point. He claimed to be the son of the Duke of Norfolk, a relationship that the nobleman had declared was news to him.

Sarah had always preferred not to think too much about the matter. When she did allow herself to do so, her best guess was that she was in actuality the manager's true daughter. Since her birth had anticipated his marriage by several months, it would have been quite in Adolphus Romney's character to weave some fanciful, romantic tale to account for this discrepancy, which he would in time come to believe himself.

''So I'm sure,'' the manager was saying, ''that when Lady Petherbridge was casting about for a suitable person to provide theatrical professionalism, while mingling comfortably with her highborn guests, she naturally thought of you.''

Refraining from pointing out the absurdity of his statement, Sarah merely asked, "But however did she learn of my existence?"

"That part should be self-evident. Did I not say when I first set eyes on the three young gentlemen in the stage box that Tidswell's fame would spread? 'O my prophetic soul!' " he declaimed once more.

Sarah, of course, had thought of that same possibility. Still, she knew of no connection between Lady Petherbridge and the threesome. But even the possibility was enough to bring a rush of embarrassment to her cheeks at the memory of her latest encounter with two of the three young swells. "I really don't think I care to go," she said diffidently, and braced for the storm of protest that was sure to break upon her head.

"Not go?" Mr. Romney surely did not hear aright. "Not go!" Mr. Romney was appalled. *"Not go!"* Mr. Romney was wounded to the soul. He talked at length about the Prodigy's career. How could that dear child's own sister stand in the way of certain patronage for Tidswell? This was the lad's big chance. With friends among the aristocracy, his meteoric rise would be the marvel of the theatrical world. Surely his sister would not be so mean-spirited as to . . . And on and on.

In the end Sarah capitulated—not for any of the reasons the manager put forward but because they were nearly destitute and the wages plus her and Tidswell's meals and lodging for a fortnight would take some of the strain off their rapidly dwindling funds.

Tidswell, though, proved even more recalcitrant than his sister. The combination of his terrifying lapse of memory in front of the Portsmouth audience followed by being set on fire had caused him to have serious second thoughts about the brilliant career his father envisioned for him. And the glowing descriptions of the grandeur of Pether Hall, gathered by Mr. Romney in various alehouses in the neighborhood, did nothing to alleviate his fears. "I ain't going," he pronounced flatly, sending his father into a fit of histrionics that made the manager's remonstrances to Sarah seem but a pale rehearsal. It was only after Tids's sister had taken the boy aside and promised he'd not have to perform unless he wished to—a promise he must not, under any circumstances, divulge to his doting father—that he finally agreed to go.

Mr. Gerard Langford considered his invitation a decided bore. His first inclination was to scrawl a reply saying that urgent business required his continued presence in the city. But upon reflection he realized the folly of offending his aunt. Besides, he thought as he frowned over the almost unintelligible communication, there might be more to it than met the eye. For his unsocial aunt to plan a house party . . . Damn it all, he'd have to go!

But despite his resolution, when he tooled his team of perfectly matched grays through the park during the fashionable hour the next day and was flagged down by Lady Scriven, who informed him that she, too, had received an invitation to Pether Hall, the instincts that had stood him in good stead in many an all-night card game made him look pityingly at the lady. "How tedious for you," he drawled. "You'll cry off, of course. I did." He smiled his slow, handsome smile, lifted his curly-brimmed beaver to the lady, nodded at her entourage of strollers, flicked his reins, and drove on, thinking furiously.

Miss Evelina Crome was as fully alarmed as Tidswell by her invitation. A shy young lady, she found the social rounds more frightening than pleasurable. And in spite of her mother's constant harping on the subject, she remained quite unconvinced of her extraordinary beauty. She saw nothing remarkable in diminutive, fragile fairness and envied the statuesque, dark goddesses of her acquaintance.

And her confidence in her appearance was not increased by her mother's constant reminders that it was her duty to trade in on it and restore the family fortunes by capturing a rich husband. Lady Emma Crome was the daughter of an impoverished nobleman and had married, as she was fond of telling her only child, quite beneath her. All of her considerable ambitions now focused on Evelina.

So when Lady Emma sailed into her daughter's bedchamber holding the Petherbridge invitation like a talisman, the young lady, who was sipping chocolate in her bed, gazed at the note with apprehension. Like Mr. Romney, she would have uttered "O my prophetic soul!" had she been acquainted with Lord Hamlet's line. "Do we have to go?" she asked timidly after she'd deciphered the scrawled message.

"What a question!" Lady Emma, who had all of the imposing stature Miss Crome envied but no claim to beauty, frowned down at her young daughter. "Do you realize who Lady Petherbridge is, my dear?" Evelina pleaded ignorance. When her mama informed her that their hostess-to-be was none other than Lord Graymarsh's aunt, her spirits plummeted even lower.

For Lord Graymarsh was the matrimonial victim her mother had targeted for her. It was useless for Evelina to point out that his lordship was the most sought-after catch on the marriage mart or to mention that he had failed to show the slightest interest in her. Her mother merely snorted with more emphasis than refinement. "Nonsense! Lord Graymarsh has never failed to stand up with you."

Though Miss Crome was certain that any number of beauties could make that claim, it would have been a waste of breath to say so. For in her own way, Lady Emma was fully as optimistic as Adolphus Romney. That she had as little basis for her sanguineness, her next utterance revealed. "Indifferent, indeed!" She scoffed at her daughter, who had allowed her chocolate to grow cold during this social crisis. "I'm convinced that Lord Graymarsh is behind the invitation. Why else would Augusta Petherbridge be asking us? Our acquaintanceship is slight." Since her daughter had no answer to this poser, Lady Emma considered the point well made. She nodded several times to underscore it and then sailed off to pen her acceptance of such a "gracious invitation."

Except for Lady Emma and possibly Randolph, the only other person who looked forward to Lady Petherbridge's house party with any degree of pleasure was the hostess. The primary purpose of the social gathering was, of course, to divert Lord Petherbridge from his doldrums. And it was already having the desired effect. If the mere anticipation of the party had so captured his attention and blotted out all thoughts of dying, just imagine the salubrious effect the event itself would have!

Lady Petherbridge had been greatly pleased when her husband had taken an interest in the guest list. When he exerted himself to the extent of wishing to know which chambers would be assigned to the various members of the party, Augusta Petherbridge's cup of happiness overflowed. To have raised her husband's spirits to this degree exceeded her fondest hopes. He made a few suggestions that she was happy to comply with, such as isolating one gentleman whose snoring could be "heard above cannon fire." So when he asked with elaborate casualness, "Where are you putting the actress and her brother?" she found nothing at all odd about the query. Her plan, she explained, had been to house them in the rooms next to the housekeeper, "between stairs," as it were.

"Won't do," his lordship said emphatically.

His wife looked up from the list with mild surprise. "Whyever not?"

"Have to treat 'em like the other guests."

"But Petherbridge, they are actors." The term might have been gypsies from the way she rolled it off her tongue.

"I know that. But you expect 'em to mingle with the guests. Ain't like they were hired to perform here on their own. They'll be acting with the others you invite. Like the Kembles do at Oatlands. Can't send out invitations, then treat the ones who get 'em like servants. Ain't done."

"But I'm paying them," his wife objected.

"The others won't know that. Ain't the thing, Gussie, not to put 'em with the guests."

Her ladyship sighed and capitulated. While she bear-led her more pliant husband in most of life's decisions, she bowed to his superior wisdom where social niceties were concerned. It all seemed rather eccentric to her mind—putting a provincial actress on the same footing with the cream of polite society, but Petherbridge undoubtedly knew best.

As for his lordship, he'd surprised himself by such uncharacteristic assertiveness. But when he mulled it over later, he was well satisfied. "Can't have me own flesh and blood treated like a servant here at Pether Hall," he muttered to himself, "no matter which side of the blanket she was born on. Wouldn't be the thing at all."

Chapter Six

Lord and Lady Petherbridge kept country hours and saw no reason to change their habits just because they were entertaining. So when the house party convened, dinner was served promptly at five, and it gave the ill-assorted guests their first opportunity to size one another up.

Lady Emma Crome had, of course, taken precedence in the march to the dining room. Miss Romney, equally of course, brought up the rear. Now, though seated figuratively below the salt, Sarah was not far enough away from that formidable dowager to escape her ladyship's inquisitive stare. The actress amused herself by attempting to read Lady Emma's mind.

The first stare had been used, Sarah felt sure, to ascertain whether the only other young lady present might prove to be a rival to her daughter. Sarah was well aware that she passed that muster—or failed, depending on the point of view. For in no way did her appearance pose any threat to the reigning beauty. It would be a rare gathering indeed, in which Miss Crome could be overshadowed. Sarah had never seen such a lovely female. But after apparently satisfying herself upon that score, Lady Emma still continued to stare down the table. It was evident that her ladyship didn't know quite what to make of Miss Sarah Romney.

Sarah was dressed in the best that the Romney costume wardrobe offered. But while her British net over blue satin frock might have given an illusion of elegance from the stage, its inferiority was immediately apparent when compared with Miss Crome's deceptively simple white muslin round dress, the work of a fashionable modiste. Lady Emma first categorized Miss Romney as a governess. But she quickly dismissed that notion as absurd. To her almost certain knowledge, the Honorable Randolph Milbanke was the youngest member of the Petherbridge connection. She mentally reran the list of possibilities and stopped on "poor relation." Yes, of course. That had to be it. Miss Romney must be one of Those.

The table conversation had ground to a halt during the first remove. Lady Emma took advantage of the lull to fasten her barrister's eye on Sarah and inquire across and down the table, "Are you perhaps related to Lord and Lady Petherbridge, Miss Romney?"

His lordship thereupon strangled on his wine and had to be pounded on the back by the nearest footman. When quiet was restored, Sarah answered clearly and politely, "No, Lady Emma. I am an actress, come to direct the theatricals."

"Indeed?" the other replied frostily, and Randolph quickly changed the subject.

The party was not as large as Sarah had expected. She looked around the table with an eye toward casting. She dismissed Lord and Lady Petherbridge as unlikely participants in the entertainment. Sir Peter Sherburne, now attacking the roasted pheasant with greedy single-mindedness, seemed equally in doubt. A gouty bachelor crony of Lord Petherbridge, Sir Peter would surprise her if he showed an inclination for performance. Nor did she have more hope for Lord and Lady Stanhope, also antiquated. No, she'd have to depend on the younger members of the group.

Sarah had been unnerved but not too surprised to find the Honorable Randolph Milbanke and Mr. Gerard Langford among the company. She had prepared herself for the possibility that her stepfather might be right for once and there could be a connection between the tonnish gentlemen of the stage box and the Petherbridge invitation. At least, she consoled herself, Lord Graymarsh wasn't present. It was embarrassing enough, meeting Mr. Langford. An encounter with the other man didn't bear thinking on.

Well, either of those two young gentlemen could play the hero's part. And despite his handsomeness, there was something decidedly villainous about Mr. Langford that assured his versatility. Nature had certainly formed Miss Crome for the perfect heroine. If only the young lady weren't so shy. Sarah sighed inwardly. She herself would be forced to take a role—or roles. She'd hoped to concentrate fully on direction. She began to regret her rash promise to Tids that he'd be exempted from performing. Still, sheer boredom might cause him to change his mind. What on earth had possessed Lady Petherbridge to ask him here? He was now dealing with a tray in his room and pretending to be a prisoner, too intimidated by the grandeur of his surroundings to venture out of the sanctuary of his bedchamber and explore the grounds as she'd suggested.

Sarah continued to study the dinner guests covertly. Her eyes darted quickly away when they reached Lord Petherbridge. Her host had been staring at her throughout the entire meal in a manner she found disconcerting. Her gaze lighted once more on Lady Emma, engrossed in conversation with Sir Peter. Her ladyship had definite dramatic possibilities. She would make, for instance, a marvelous witch for the opening of *Macbeth*. If only there were a few more people here to choose from . . .

Sarah proved not to be the only one whose mind was on the guest list. "I'm sorry your friend Lady Scriven could not join us," Lady Petherbridge said abruptly to Mr. Langford.

"Oh, was Lucy asked here?" Gerard inquired innocently. "Pity she couldn't come."

"Wrote she had a putrid throat," his aunt informed him.

"Glad she didn't come, then." Sir Peter spoke through a mouthful of prawns. "Very catching, putrid throats."

Lady Stanhope shuddered and launched into a recital of the various times she'd succumbed to the same illness.

"I didn't know Lady Scriven was ailing. Did you, Gerry?" Randolph seemed suspicious.

"That I did not." The guileless blue eyes met his cousin's stare. "I must have a posy sent around."

"And speaking of persons who ain't here"—Lord Petherbridge entered the conversation suddenly—"what's keeping Gray?"

The query shattered the calm of the two young ladies present. They had both breathed private sighs of relief at the baron's absence.

"Oh, is Lord Graymarsh expected?" Lady Emma could not conceal her delight at this bit of news. "Such a charming young man. So attentive to my Evelina at her come-out. Put the dear child quite at ease."

Sarah doubted that. She stole a look at the beauty and felt a pang of sympathy as the girl's face flamed red.

"Oh, yes. My cousin is noted for his attention to young ladies." Gerard smiled his enigmatic smile at Sarah, who willed herself not to engage Miss Crome in a blushing contest.

"Don't know what's gotten into the boy." Petherbridge clung to his train of thought. "Used to be the soul of punctuality. Now it seems as if he's late for everything." A terrible notion struck him. "You don't suppose he's coming by balloon," he said to the world at large.

"Don't be ridiculous, Petherbridge." His wife disposed of that subject and turned back with martyred resignation to her duty as hostess as Lady Stanhope exhausted putrid throats and moved on to the history of her frequent megrims, sparing no detail.

At the end of the interminable meal, it was decided that the guests would take a garden stroll, then afterward enjoy their tea in a lakeside pagoda. Sarah took advantage of the interval required for the gentlemen to enjoy their port to go and rescue her little brother. She neither knew nor cared whether it was proper to include Tids in the outing. She only knew that he could not remain cowering in his room for an entire fortnight. They joined the group as the party was leaving the house by way of the conservatory.

It was obvious that Tidswell's presence did little to enhance Sarah's social status. That fact perturbed her not at all. What did disturb her was the way he quaked under the censorious stare of Lady Emma. To offset his fear, she took him firmly by the hand, a state of affairs he would have fiercely resisted under less intimidating circumstances.

As the group began its promenade around an artificial lake, the younger members of the party soon outstripped their elders, who were inclined to take advantage of the various seats and rotundas that they passed. Away from at least that much intimidation, Tids shook off Sarah's hand. He looked back over his shoulder at the imposing stone exterior of Pether Hall reflected in all its formal symmetry in the lake. He gazed around him at the seemingly endless expanse of garden whose "natural" vistas belied the army of gardeners and the hours of work needed to create them.

Tidswell began to feel that he was fortunate to be there after all. He paused a moment on an arched bridge that crossed a narrow finger of the lake to gaze at some fishes swimming there, marking them for a return engagement with a fishing pole. As he caught up with the other strollers, he fell into step with Miss Evelina Crome, much to his sister's astonishment.

Instinctively, Tids had recognized someone at least as intimidated by their circumstances as he was. Under Eveline's shy and lovely gaze, he began to lose his inhibitions and to revert to his natural ebullient state. She too seemed to forget her self-consciousness and giggled like a schoolgirl, when an enraged goose he'd paused to tease came hissing out of the water after him. Even Mr. Langford dropped his world-weary pose and smiled at the beauty's infectious laughter.

Now that she'd ceased to worry about Tidswell, Sarah was puzzling over the behavior of the two gentlemen. To her way of thinking, their conduct defied all logic. Ignoring the beauty, they had attached themselves to her. She could better understand Randolph's actions. He seemed a kind young gentleman who would go out of his way to make a social inferior feel at ease. But she was unable to think the same of Mr. Langford. Self-interest seemed to be his guiding principle. So why he, who could barely suppress a shudder at the dowdiness of her gown, should be vying with his cousin to entertain her was certainly perplexing. Especially when Miss Crome was in the party.

True, Miss Crome's mother was enough to put off any number of potential suitors, Sarah thought, but still . . . She stiffened suddenly as she recalled that compromising situation Mr. Langford had recently interrupted. If he, like his odious cousin, thought for one minute that she was the kind of young woman he could count on to take the tedium away from a boring party—well, he was in for a bit of disillusionment. She gave the elegant gentleman, who was walking unnecessarily close to her, a telling look. Gerard was astute enough to take her meaning and turned to enter Tids and Miss Crome's discussion of the delights of country fairs.

Sarah was glad to see Tidswell enjoying himself, but she almost wished he'd not come out of his shell quite so far. He now held center stage. And Sarah was suddenly aware of the Yorkshire overtones in her brother's voice. Mr. Romney came from the north, and the company had spent a great deal of time there. Sarah's stint in Miss Marshall's Academy for Young Ladies, plus the natural ear invaluable to an actress, had left her speech free of the regional dialect that now seemed so out of place. If Tids did fulfill his father's dream of Drury Lane, he was destined to play the rustic, Sarah thought as her little brother considered aloud the possibility of mastering the sword-swallower's technique he'd witnessed at a fair and including it in his own performance.

Mr. Langford thought it an excellent notion. "Your *Merchant of Venice* recitation seems an ideal time to swallow something," he offered. "During the first scene, don't you think?"

Just as Tids had worked out that he was being insulted and was wracking his brain for a setdown that would take some starch out of the puffed-up swell, Miss Crome made her first contribution to the general conversation. "Oh, my goodness, what is that?" She craned her pretty neck and squinted skyward.

Outlined against a vivid blue background and floating among powder puffs of clouds was a small, spherical object that had absolutely no business being there. It came from the northeast and moved toward them slowly, catching the reflected rays of the low-lying sun like a mirror flashing signals, causing the gaping observers to shade their eyes with their hands in an effort to identify the heavenly body.

"Lord save us!" There was terror in the Prodigy's voice.

"It's a meteor from outer space, and it's headed straight for us!"

"At a celestial snail's-pace? Don't be sap-skulled," Mr. Langford drawled.

The phenomenon shifted slightly in the breeze then, and whatever there was about it that was picking up sunbeams with such blinding intensity went out of focus, and the object, though still small and distant, lost its mystery and became easily discernible.

"It's a balloon!" Master Tidswell whooped.

"Oh, my God, Gray!" His lordship's brother groaned.

"What a bore." His cousin brought his quizzing glass into play and gazed skyward with distaste.

"Do you mean that's actually Lord Graymarsh?" Sarah stared with horrified fascination as the balloon drifted inexorably their way. It was now possible to see its metallic silver coloring and the band of crimson-bordered blue that encircled its circumference like a broad equator. "Surely it can't be!"

"Bound to be him." Randolph sighed. "Can't think of anybody else around here queer enough in the attic to be flying one of the things. For the past six months, it's been all he thinks of. Bound to break his neck one of these days. Oh, it's Gray all right."

"How awful!" Miss Crome's murmur was so heartfelt as to cause the others to switch their attention from the balloon to her. It was hard to tell whether the exclamation was for Lord Graymarsh's peril or his imminent arrival.

The balloon, still headed in their direction, seemed to be sinking rapidly. It was now possible to make out the rope netting that covered the silk cylinder and to at least identify the lone figure in the boat dangling beneath it as a dark-haired male. The Prodigy was suddenly overcome by excitement and began to jump up and down, waving both arms ecstatically. "Oh, I say, this is famous!" he crowed repeatedly. The figure in the boat obligingly waved back.

"My God, would you look at that." Even Mr. Langford was forced to mutter a grudging tribute to his cousin's navigational skills. Gray was obviously controlling his descent rate versus his projected distance with a mind toward landing on the grassy, level expanse just beyond them. It was possible now to get a good view of the aeronaut as he intently worked his valves, letting the air escape in properly controlled amounts to guarantee a safe and accurate meeting with terra firma. But just as Randolph and Tidswell broke into spontaneous huzzahs, a sudden, capricious breeze sprang up and focused like a bellows upon the deflating silk. The gust changed the balloon's direction and aimed it straight at the watchers.

"Get down!" Mr. Langford yelled, then saw to it that his command was at least in part obeyed by the simple expedient of snatching Miss Crome off her feet and flattening her beside him on the turf. The others dived in similar fashion just as the blue and crimson boat sailed over the space where moments before their heads had been.

"Bloody hell!" Lord Graymarsh was heard to say as he floated gracefully over five prone bodies and headed toward the lake.

Chapter Seven

The walking party scrambled to their feet, then stood like the monoliths at Stonehenge as the balloon continued its capricious descent and came to rest, like a huge swan settling, near the center of the lake. The gossamer silk balloon, almost deflated, stayed aloft, breeze-held, for a second, then with a soft, rustling sigh, floated downward to meet the rippling water.

"Come on, Gerry!" Randolph had shrugged out of his formfitting evening coat and was hopping on one foot when his cousin laid a restraining hand upon his shoulder.

"Don't be such a gudgeon." Mr. Langford spoke reprovingly. "Gray's a better swimmer than either one of us."

"Yes, but he's underneath that damned balloon and he could have hurt himself."

Randolph had succeeded in ridding himself of his black slippers and would have leaped into the lake except for the firm grip that held him. "No need for both of you to take a ducking, you know."

"Dammit, let me go!" Randolph was growing frantic. He leveled a punch in the direction of his cousin's jaw that the star pupil of Cribb's Parlour had no difficulty dodging.

"Look there, you hothead." Gerard nodded toward the water. "If you want to spoil your clothing, go ahead. God knows it's no great loss to the world of fashion. Who does make your shirts? But as I predicted, your heroics will be ridiculously misplaced."

Just as the silk descended to obscure him, Gray had dived out of the boat. He'd shrugged out of his jacket and kicked off his boots, glumly wondering what his valet would have to say over the second outfit ruined in a fortnight's time. Though tempted to turn toward the bank opposite his watchers, he decided that that would be too craven. He regretted not having taken the coward's way, however, when he pulled himself, dripping, out of the water and confirmed the fleeting impression he'd registered from his bird's-eye view of the figures throwing themselves upon the ground. Miss Sarah Romney was indeed among them. She was now staring at him with a face free of all expression but with disapproval written largely in her luminous blue eyes.

Sarah might have been the only person present. "I had not expected to find you at Pether Hall, Miss Romney," Lord Graymarsh said formally, while at the same time he peeled a water lily petal, which clung like a mustard plaster, off his thigh.

"Nor I, you," she replied haughtily. "But in your case, Pether Hall is the mildest of the unexpected possibilities. I had not expected to see you flying overhead. Or playing Triton the sea god rising from the water, when it comes to that."

"Sea god, Miss Romney?" Gerard gazed at his dripping cousin. "Wouldn't beached mackerel be more accurately descriptive? Really, Gray, this habit of yours of coming to light in awkward places is the outside of enough. First a bog. Now a lake. Is there some balloonist's rule against landing on solid ground?"

His lordship grinned sheepishly, accepted the handkerchief his brother offered, and began to wipe the streaming water from his face and eyes.

What had happened to the cool, elegant fashionplate she had first seen at the Portsmouth Theatre and found so disconcertingly attractive? Miss Romney asked herself. That sophisticated image was fading rapidly; superimposed, perhaps forever, was this second view of Lord Graymarsh in dishabille. So tightly was his linen plastered to his torso that he might have been shirtless once again. His pantaloons, close-fitting due to his tailor's art, now served as a second skin. Sarah glanced at Miss Crome just then and found that she was blushing. Her eyes were demurely averted from what might as well have been his lordship in the raw. Sarah was caught off guard by an almost uncontrollable desire to giggle. Fortunately for her dignity, the Prodigy suddenly redirected the group's attention. "How long do you think it will stay afloat?" he asked anxiously, his troubled gaze intent on the mass of silk floating in the water.

"That's a good question," Gray answered grimly. "I think the boat's fairly watertight. But a soaking won't do the balloon much good. At any rate, I'd better round up some help and get it out while there's still light enough to see by."

"Don't look at me, old boy." Mr. Langford yawned. "Pulling balloons out of lakes holds little appeal for me. Besides, we're due at the pagoda for tea."

"I'm sure he wasn't expecting any exertion on your part." Randolph's voice dripped acid. "My God, Gray, it was Portsmouth Theatre all over again. Anybody who wants to can burn up or drown before our cousin will risk rumpling the cravat it took him forty minutes before a looking glass to tie.'' By lashing out at his relative, the young man was finding release for the scare he'd just been given.

''Forty minutes? You malign me. I assure you that I can, on my better days, achieve the perfection of the Langford fall in less than twenty. Only a clutch-fist would require forty.''

''Oh, the devil with your deuced neckcloth. That ain't the point, and you know it. The point is, you weren't about to put yourself out to rescue Gray.''

From Randolph's point of view that might have been the main thrust of his tirade. But from the manner in which the two Romneys were staring at Mr. Langford, it was evident that they had not missed the oblique reference to the Portsmouth Theatre. As far as they were both concerned, Mr. Langford's action—or lack of it—there was the only point.

That astute gentleman took note of their reaction. ''I never believe in unnecessary exertion, dear Coz.'' Gerard's tone was careless, but the look he bent on Randolph was filled with venom. Whether or not his cousin had intended to alienate Miss Romney was a moot point. The fact remained that he'd dealt Mr. Langford's pursuit of the heiress a severe blow. ''At Portsmouth, Gray here had the young thespian's cloak off before, alas, I'd become aware anything was amiss. Did the same not apply to you? As I recall, you arrived on stage as tardily as I.'' He noted that some of the Romneys' hostility was fading. ''And just why,'' he continued, ''you thought I should immerse myself in that filthy lake to keep Gray company is more than I can fathom. Surely he can make a private cake of himself without turning it into a family affair. My only regret in this sordid episode is that I prevented you from joining him. Your hot head could use some cooling.''

''Stop it, you two.'' Dripping wet or not, the baron

sounded every inch a lord. "Randolph, I take it that you wish to help. Would you round up some gardeners? Tell them to fetch a boat. In the meantime, Gerry, you might escort the ladies and, er, Master Tidswell on to tea."

Randolph loped off on his mission, but the Prodigy's face fell. "Oh, can't I stay and watch? I don't want any old tea, and I've never seen a balloon pulled out of a lake before. I'd like to above all things. Is it all right if I stay, Sarah?"

"Certainly." His sister enjoyed overruling their imperious dismissal and annoying Lord Graymarsh. "I think I should like to see the rescue myself. Miss Crome, will you not join us? I'm sure Mr. Langford will make our excuses to the others." Seating herself upon the grass as though settling in for a Vauxhall Gardens spectacle, Sarah didn't bother to suppress a smile at the disgusted look on his lordship's face. She didn't mind at all that he knew she was enjoying his discomfort.

Torn between embarrassment at his lordship's revealing dampness and the prospect of strolling alone with Mr. Langford, who made her even more uncomfortable, Miss Crome elected to remain. For she was quite certain that Lady Emma would wish her to hold her position near Lord Graymarsh, despite his shocking state, rather than to walk unaccompanied with his slightly scandalous cousin. So after placing a dainty handkerchief on the grass, she sat down beside Miss Romney. "Yes, I think I should like to see the balloon rescued, too," she said, though without much conviction in her voice.

"I'm aware that Pether Hall is hardly the Royal Pavilion," Graymarsh remarked dryly, "but I didn't expect my uncle's guests to be this hard up for entertainment."

"Didn't you?" Gerard answered. "Can't have thought much about it, then; that's obvious. Well, if beauty has elected to stay here," he said with a sigh, "I hesitate to join the crones. I except your mother from that general description, of course, Miss Crome. Still, one hates to forgo one's tea for the dubious excitement of seeing several soaking yards of silk pulled from brackish water. By George, I have it! We'll have tea brought here. Young Tidswell!" The Prodigy turned from trying to ascertain whether more of the balloon had become submerged than when he'd looked a second earlier and eyed the starchy cove warily. "I don't suppose you could be bribed to go tell the servants to— Never mind." He abandoned the notion before the lad's look of horror. "They'd never do anything on your say-so, anyhow. What a bore. I'll have to go myself. Don't do anything till I get back, Gray. The rescue of your balloon, I'm sure, will quite eclipse Miss Romney's theatricals for excitement and suspense." He bowed to the ladies and set off at a leisurely pace to retrace their footsteps along the gravel path.

The Prodigy joined the two ladies on the grass and continued his anxious balloon surveillance. Lord Graymarsh stood awkwardly, pulling covertly at his clinging shirt and breeches. He felt more uncomfortable than at almost any point in his memory. Certainly more than at any point in his entire adult life. And he had no problem accounting for his loss of poise.

Its cause was not the young beauty whose cheeks flamed with embarrassment and who could not bring herself to look at him directly. As always, he felt only sympathy for Miss Crome. He was well aware that her dragon of a mother was determined that the beauty bring him to heel and lead him to the altar. He also realized that Evelina was more terrified of succeeding in that Herculean task than she was of failure. When Lady Emma had maneuvered him into standing up with her daughter for the second time at the girl's come-out, he'd thought, Why doesn't the old witch find some nice young squire at home for her? He was usually adept at sidestepping such manipulation. But the desire to save Miss Crome from a scold about her shyness overrode his judgment. Now, as he looked at the girl's flushed cheeks, he wished that he'd squelched that kindly impulse. He'd only managed to stoke the fires of her mother's high ambition. Hence their presence at Pether Hall. Gray wondered if his cousin's fine Italian hand was behind their invitation. It never occurred to him that his little brother would set such a trap for him.

No, it was not Miss Crome's presence that was discomforting to his lordship. He could live with her averted eyes. It was the mockery in the beautiful blue eyes of the other female and the suppressed laughter that caused her tightly pursed mouth to betray itself ever so slightly now and then in the beginnings of a grin that made him long to snatch her up and toss her headlong into the lake. To prevent himself from possibly doing the unthinkable and also to break the weighty silence, he remarked, "I believe my cousin mentioned something about theatricals, Miss Romney."

"Yes, I believe he did," she replied gravely, then loosed the threatened grin as his lordship, upon shifting his position slightly, gave a sudden hop. The suppressed giggle broke free of all restraint as Gray stood on one leg like a stork and pulled a burr off the sole of his wet and muddy stocking.

"You will, I take it, be performing, then?" he asked between clenched teeth.

"Directing, at any rate." She choked back the laughter under the full force of his glare. "Lady Petherbridge has *hired* me"—Miss Crome gave her a startled glance as Sarah emphasized the word—"to help entertain her houseguests. I do hope that explains my presence here sufficiently. I can see it puzzles you. Did you think, perhaps, I was here on your account?"

"No. You quite mistake the matter. Believe me, I have not concerned myself about the whys and wherefores of your being here."

"Fustian!" Sarah replied pleasantly. "You might have seen a ghost when you floundered out of the lake."

"Floundered?" He looked dangerous.

"Whatever. I do not expect you to believe this, sir. I offer it merely for the record. I had no idea that you were connected in any way with Lady Petherbridge. Not that such knowledge would have kept me away," she added in a burst of candor. "No matter how I may have wished it otherwise, I fear that the proffered wage would have outweighed even my desire to avoid your lordship. The Romney Company is down on its luck, you see."

Miss Crome looked ready to faint at such plain speaking. And his lordship was regretting not having stayed on board his doomed balloon in the noble tradition of sea captains, when the Prodigy, who had paid no attention to his elders' conversation, exclaimed with distressed single-mindedness, "Oh, I do wish they'd hurry. I'm scared it's going to sink."

In spite of a growing desire to strangle the boy's sister, Graymarsh was moved by the Prodigy's concern. "No, I think it will be all right. The boat should float forever."

"It will soon be dark, though." It occurred to Gray to wonder if the loss of the balloon wouldn't pain the lad at least as much as it would bother him. The Prodigy's next speech erased all doubt. "I never saw anything to touch it," the boy confided in an embarrassed rush. "Just floating through the sky like a bird. A big silver bird. It was famous, sir. The prettiest sight I've ever seen. There you were, floating up there in the heavens just like you belonged. I can just picture what it must be like. Why, looking down on all the poor creatures stuck tight to the ground must make you feel like a god or something. It must be the grandest feeling in the world."

"It is all of that." Gray was looking at Tidswell with new respect and thinking how much more appealing the eager face and shining eyes seemed now in the grip of real emotion than in all the posturing and swaggering upon the stage. He smiled at the boy. ''When we get the balloon out of the lake and have it sufficiently dried out, would you like to see for yourself? Go up in it, I mean?''

''Oh, sir, could I really?'' Tidswell could hardly contain himself. ''You ain't bamming me, are you, sir? Of course I'd like it. I'd like it above all things. I'd like it more than—''

''No!'' The word rolled off Miss Romney's tongue with dramatic force and echoed across the water. She had leaped to her feet and was staring at the two enthusiasts with horror. ''Tidswell, you are not even to consider such a possibility. The idea is unthinkable. I forbid it! Absolutely!''

''You wouldn't do that. You couldn't!'' Her brother turned toward her, aghast. His voice was choked. ''You don't even know what you're saying.''

''I certainly do know.'' In the face of his obvious distress, Sarah tried to soften her strident tone. ''I'm well aware of the dangers of ballooning. And I'm also aware that our father would never consent to your doing such a foolhardy thing and would completely disown me if I allowed it.''

''But Sarah!'' The Prodigy's wail was stricken. It came from his very soul.

''I hope your lordship is satisfied.'' She directed her bitterness to where it belonged. ''Break your own neck if you've a mind to, but pray, sir, leave my brother out of your harebrained schemes.''

''Thank you for your kind permission, but I've no intention of breaking my neck or anybody else's. I assure you there's very little danger in balloon flight.''

''Oh, yes. I'm sure it's perfectly safe.'' Her tone was withering. ''You made that abundantly clear when you chose to bring your craft down in the middle of the lake. Why, you might just as well have landed in a treetop—or on a church steeple, or in the channel, or—or—'' She sputtered to a close, more from a threatening fit of apoplexy than from the fact that she'd exhausted the list of dire possibilities.

"Trust an actress to make a Cheltenham tragedy out of a simple balloon ride," Gray remarked to the world at large, then, to the Prodigy, "I'm sorry for your sister's prejudice. Though I'm not surprised at such a reaction from a female."

"A female!" Miss Romney choked. "Some of the world's foremost balloonists have been females, I'll have you know. And died for their pioneering. Sex has nothing to say to anything."

His lordship ignored that and addressed the boy. "As I was about to say, since you are not of age, I'm afraid I can't take you up in opposition to your sister's wishes."

Tidswell glared at Sarah, then burst into tears.

"Oh, thank you very much." The actress looked daggers at the nobleman.

"But if, on the other hand," Gray continued, "your father were to grant that permission—well, that would be another matter, would it not?"

"Divide and conquer?" Sarah inquired.

"Certainly not. I just hate to see a fellow enthusiast suffer from a stupid, baseless prejudice, that's all."

"All? Is that all, indeed?" she began but, fortunately perhaps, was prevented from elaborating by the simultaneous arrival of the tea and the rescue team.

Rescue came by water in the form of two flatboats. One headed directly toward the center of the lake while the other made for shore, where his lordship stood impatiently waiting for it. Since he'd not begun the drying process enough to matter, he waded in to help the burly punter nose his boat onto land so that Randolph could climb out.

"You're sure you don't need my help?" Randolph eyed the baskets that two footmen were placing on the grass.

"No, have your tea."

His brother's testy voice gave Randolph second thoughts. "Wouldn't dream of deserting you in your hour of need," he pronounced stoutly. "Let's shove off."

"Don't be such a gudgeon." Gray managed a weak smile in lieu of saying that Randolph was in no way responsible for his irritation. "I'm grateful to you for fetching help. I'd have hated to trudge the distance stocking-footed. Go on now." He held the boat steady so that his brother could climb out, then jumped in himself. The gardener pushed off.

"Oh, I say, sir." Tidswell was too embarrassed by his recent tears to manage more than a mumble. But fortunately his lordship heard and told the punter to hold up. "Would you like to come along, Tids?" he called back over his shoulder.

"Oh, could I, sir?"

"Certainly. I should have thought to ask you." Without even glancing Miss Romney's way for her permission, Gray jumped into the water, which was waist-high, and waded to the shore. "Climb on my back," he commanded, kneeling down. "And for God's sake, keep your feet up. I don't want to be held responsible if you soak your boots."

Tidswell followed his instructions to the letter and was deposited into the flatboat high and dry. The craft rocked dangerously as Gray pulled himself up over the side, but a shift of balance by the gardener soon steadied it. They moved rapidly toward the other boat as the shadows lengthened across the lake.

In the meantime, the footmen had spread a linen tablecloth upon the grass and had distributed china, silver, napkins, and mounds of cakes. After a second's indecision, the silver teapot had been placed before Miss Romney, the senior of the ladies. The footmen then retired to a respectful distance to allow the alfresco party to have the semblance of privacy even as they watched discreetly in case something was required.

"Well," Mr. Langford remarked indifferently as he accepted a Dresden cup from Miss Romney's hand, "I see that the fleet has arrived in time. The imperiled vessel will be towed to dock."

"I wish it would sink like a stone."

"Surely, Miss Romney, you don't really mean that." Randolph spoke through a mouthful of cake.

"Oh, do I not! Lord Graymarsh has offered Tidswell a ride in the horrid thing. And I've forbidden my brother to set one foot inside that hanging coffin. Nothing but a watery grave for that curst balloon will save Tids and me from the worst—indeed, I think the only—row of our entire lives."

Mr. Langford gazed toward the center of the lake. "It pains me, then, to inform you that it appears they've worked out a salvage plan. The modus operandi seems to involve placing the collapsed balloon in one flatboat and allowing its carrier to trail behind, while pulling the two in tandem with the other. Oh, I say, your little brother seems to have decided to climb into the balloon boat."

"Oh, bother!" Sarah scrambled to her feet to confirm this, wondering what had become of Graymarsh's concern for Tidswell's best boots. "It's bound to leak."

"Well, at least now he can say he's had a balloon ride," Randolph remarked.

"Think that will satisfy him?" Mr. Langford asked the question without much interest.

"Of course it won't," Tidswell's sister retorted. "It will only serve to whet his appetite. Oh, blast his lordship for a villain! A 'bloody, bawdy villain! Remorseless, treacherous, lecherous, kindless villain!' " The Shakespearean oaths came tripping off her tongue. She might have been the Romney Company manager at his most fulsome.

"Miss Romney!" Miss Crome gasped. At first she looked shocked at Sarah's tirade, then she suddenly broke into a spontaneous peal of laughter that caused the other three to turn and stare. Stripped of her shyness, the beauty had never looked more appealing. Randolph's eyes widened, as if really seeing her for the first time. Gerard, in the act of taking snuff, paused halfway to his nose. "Miss Romney, you are a caution." Evelina chortled. "I've never met anyone so divertingly original. Just imagine calling Lord Graymarsh a 'bawdy villain'! And all the rest of it! I vow, my m-mother would expire to hear you. However do you manage to think up these things?"

"I really couldn't say," Miss Romney answered levelly, while Mr. Langford's snuff, inhaled too quickly, sent him into a sneezing, coughing fit. "The words just seem to come to me."

Later that evening, when the members of the house party had retired, Randolph made his way to his cousin's chamber carrying a candle that trailed a smoke line in the drafty hall. He found Gerard, clad in a magnificent gold brocade dressing gown, propped up in bed with Byron's latest volume discarded at his side while he slowly sipped from a crystal wineglass. Uninvited, Randolph helped himself to the decanter and pulled up a chair. The other man frowned. "Prepared for a coze, are you?" he asked pointedly.

"Yes. Wanted to get your opinion on our progress."

"Progress? In what respect? I wasn't aware that we'd made any. Unless you call surviving one full day of our aunt's tedious hospitality progress. Which is a point, I suppose." He took another appreciative sip. "Uncle's cellar is the only bright spot in a dull prospect, Randolph, so please do not toss your wine off in that oafish manner. Savor it like a gentleman."

"Dammit, Gerry, don't try your poses on me. I know you too well by half. You know perfectly well what kind of progress I'm talking about. Progress with Miss Romney. But you did speak the truth without meaning to: you and I ain't made any. At least not so far as I can tell. There's one good thing, though. Gray's definitely been eliminated. That's something positive to drink to, anyhow.'' He misread the other man's speaking look as he stretched his long legs in a forty-five-degree angle and rested his slippers on the white coverlet. He had left his coat back in his room. To add to his comfort, he unwound his elaborate cravat.

''Staying long?'' his cousin murmured.

''Oh, I know what you're thinking.'' Randolph ignored the interruption and kept a single-minded grip on his train of thought. ''Gray was already out of the competition. That's what he gave us to believe, at any rate.''

''And you doubted it?'' Gerard asked sarcastically.

''Oh, I didn't doubt that he believed it at the time. Pursuing a female without her having the slightest notion why goes against the grain with Gray. I know him well enough to be sure of that. Don't like it above half myself. But I rather thought that in spite of what he said he was attracted to Miss Romney. She's surprisingly likable, ain't she?'' He spoke with obvious relief, and his cousin nodded. ''And I was sure that she was taken with him. Females generally are. And that rescue thing at the theater made him the odds-on favorite. But she's really turned against him since he offered the Prodigy a ride in his balloon. He couldn't have done us a bigger favor if he'd planned for days just how to go about it.''

''You think so?'' His cousin's look was enigmatic.

''I know so. Miss Romney really has it in for my brother now.'' He chuckled as he took a gulp of wine. ''For God's sake, Gerry, weren't you listening? Didn't you hear all those different kinds of villains that she called him? By the by, whichever of us wins Miss Romney in the end should have a private word with her on that sort of thing. All right for the stage, perhaps, but won't do in the polite world. But that's neither here nor there just now. The point I'm making is, no matter how smitten Miss Romney may have been at first, Gray's really managed to get himself in her black book. She actually detests him now!" crowed his lordship's brother.

Randolph paused for a response from his other rival. When none came, he gave vent to his exasperation. "There's no use looking so Friday-faced, Gerard. Come on, admit it. You're as relieved as I am that Miss Romney's take a violent dislike to Gray."

"Oh, no, you're wrong there, Coz. I am not relieved at all. And if you are, as you claim, it only goes to show that you have a lot yet to learn about the other sex. Now if Miss Romney were indifferent to your brother, *then* I'd be relieved. But that she despises him? Frankly, I find that sufficient reason for alarm." He yawned elaborately.

"Oh." The wind was obviously leaving Randolph's sails. He did not for a moment question his cousin's superior knowledge of the female nature. Gerard had been on the town too long for Randolph to doubt his insights. But after a moment's silence, the resilient young man brightened. "Well, there's still Miss Crome."

"Ah, yes. The fair Evelina."

"Her mama wants Gray for her."

"You noticed that."

Randolph ignored the sarcasm. "He could do worse, you know," he continued thoughtfully. "Oh, I didn't think so at first. For in spite of Miss Crome's being the prettiest female I've ever seen, bar none, I thought her insipid, didn't you?"

"Shy is the term I might have used."

"But I think that if you could get her away from her odious mother long enough she'd be a different person. Don't you agree?"

"The possibility has occurred to me."

"I mean, did you see her when she was laughing at Miss Romney? I found her quite a taking little thing. Didn't you think so, Gerry?"

"I suppose my reaction could be so described."

"So even if what you say is true, about Miss Romney's not being indifferent to Gray, I mean, I think Miss Crome—and her mother—can be counted on to cut him from the competition. And you can thank me for that, Gerry. It was my idea to have Aunt Augusta ask 'em."

"So I surmised. And I also gather it was your idea to invite Lady Scriven to join our happy gathering." Gerard's eyes narrowed.

Randolph grinned sheepishly. "Well, yes, as a matter of fact, it was. You can't actually blame me, now can you? I ain't a complete ninnyhammer, you know. I realize any female's bound to prefer you or Gray to me. So I thought it a rather good notion to keep you both occupied. Too bad Lady Scriven had to go and develop a putrid throat."

"Checkmate, Coz."

"You mean you put her off? Damnation. Well, one out of two ain't all that bad. At least I've flung Miss Crome at Gray's head. A pity the girl ain't rich."

"Why? That should make no difference where Gray's concerned."

"I know. But I wouldn't mind dangling after the beauty myself now." Randolph heaved a heavy sigh. "Lord, I'd give a monkey not to be required to find an heiress. It's dashed inconvenient not having a fortune of one's own."

"You don't say so." The bitterness in Gerard's voice caused his cousin to look up sharply. But he was met by the usual lazy smile. "Do go to bed, Randolph," Mr. Langford said with a dismissive gesture. "One needs one's rest. How else to face the tedium of the morrow?"

Chapter Eight

M*iss Romney woke up early and tapped softly on Tids*well's door. It was opened almost immediately by the Prodigy, who was dressed in oversized buckskins and riding boots. Sarah had fared slightly better from the same costume source. Her slate-colored, braid-trimmed riding dress, while of inferior cut and cloth, had at least been sized for her. "I don't think anyone's up yet," she whispered. But to safeguard the secrecy of their departure, they stole down the servants' stairs.

As Sarah had hoped, in his mounting excitement Tidswell seemed to forget his balloon grievances as they approached the stables. "Are you sure the nobs won't care?" he asked anxiously.

"Don't say nobs, Tids. Lord Petherbridge made it quite clear that his guests should use his horses."

"Yes, but I'll bet a monkey he took it for granted that everybody knew how to ride."

"Undoubtedly. That's why I wanted us to practice before we're asked to join in some excursion. There was talk last night about exploring the scenic areas in the neighborhood."

"And do you think they'll have a hunt?"

"I've no idea. But I certainly hope not."

"I think it would be famous," her brother crowed. "Riding to hounds! Jumping fences!"

"Don't get above yourself. We'll do well to manage a sedate pace."

"Well, it can't be all that hard. Seems to me the horse does all the real work."

In actuality it proved far more difficult than Tids had predicted. Sarah ordered the horses saddled with a careless assurance that caused the stable boy to overestimate greatly her ability. The mount he brought her, though schooled to carry ladies, was by no means a plodder. And when the Prodigy requested a "prime goer," the groom, barely Tidswell's senior, was willing to comply.

He stood by to watch them mount, an act that Sarah, with her stage training, had observed closely and now tried to imitate. But the horse she had watched hadn't persisted in going around and around in circles. Finally aboard, and noting that Tids had also reached the saddle after several abortive tries, she then declined the groom's rather anxious offer to accompany them. Under the stable boy's doubtful gaze, Sarah clucked to her mount, a technique gleaned from observing Lord Petherbridge the day before. Nothing happened. She tried again, this time with more success. The mare turned her head and looked at the groom in protest.

Observing his sister's problems, Tidswell varied her technique. Along with the prescribed cluck, he dug his heels into his horse's flanks. Results were instantaneous.

His mount shot off. And Sarah's mare, at last realizing what was expected of it, immediately followed suit.

The Prodigy's instinct for self-preservation wiped out his sister's lectures on equestrian skill. He flung himself forward, his stomach rattling on his horse's back, and somehow managed to fling his arms around the creature's neck. Screeching bloody murder all the while, Tids hung on for all that he was worth.

Sarah was not so fortunate. As her horse, panicked by Tids's screams, broke into a gallop, her instincts were to wrap herself, Tids-style, as close to the animal's hide as possible. But her lady's saddle prevented this procedure. As it was, her knee, crooked around the pommel, acted as an axis. This focal point remained a constant as she bounced around, teeth rattling, spine jarring upward through her skull, never alighting in the same spot twice. How she and the horse remained tenuously united defied all natural laws. On one bound, she dipped so far over to the side that her head paralleled the ground they were flying over. With a mighty effort, she saved herself from falling and struggled upright, only to be immediately flung backward where her head rattled on the horse's croup. If I survive this ride, she thought, my future is assured. Astley's Royal Circus is bound to find a spot for me. Just then an especially hearty jolt helped Sarah gain a more or less upright position once again. They were speeding across a meadow now. And while she bounced erratically, like a backward toddler's first rubber ball, Sarah observed three things: that her horse and Tids's mount still maintained the same distance ratio they'd started with; that they were running pell-mell toward a patch of woods; and that they had been joined in their headlong gallop by another rider.

Even as her rattling teeth connected with her tongue, even in her shocking state of terror, even as she dipped perilously close to the horse's side once more, Sarah still managed to feel a rush of indignation that it was Tidswell whom Lord Graymarsh was intent on saving and not her.

It was a near thing altogether. When Gray, out for an early-morning ride, had seen two horses flying across the meadow, his first reaction had been annoyance for the end of his solitude. Then, as the mounts drew nearer with unnerving speed, he mentally cursed the two fools for their neck-or-nothing race. But when they drew close enough for him to see one rider plastered like a poultice on his charger's back and the other rattling around like errant hail, he woke up to the fact that he was witnessing two runaways. He knew that once the horses reached the woods, both riders were going to be scraped off the horses' backs like barnacles from a ship's hull. He dug his heels into his mount and rode like the very devil.

Gray approached Tidswell at a ninety-degree angle that forced the Prodigy's horse to swerve just before it reached disaster. He managed to chase the maddened animal down and then clutch its bridle, meanwhile yelling to the boy, "Stop your caterwauling. This poor beast's panicked!"

"H-he's panicked!" Tids wailed, his terror overridden now by bitterness as his horse decreased its pace. "How the deuce does he think I feel?" The Prodigy didn't wait for a complete cessation of all movement. A normal canter was good enough. He rolled off the creature's back and hit the ground with a grateful thud.

Sarah's horse, she had discovered, had no character of its own. A natural follower, it had swerved after Tidswell's mount. It now came thundering toward its stable companion with Sarah shouting "Whoa! Whoa! Whoa!" in a voice fit more for lament than for equestrian direction.

But in its first independent action of the day, the mare declined to rendezvous and dashed on by the others. Cursing like the cavalryman he wasn't, Lord Graymarsh set off in hot pursuit. Once again he was able to catch hold of a bridle and slow a terrified animal down. "There, there, old girl, everything's all right.'' He clucked soothingly. ''No need to panic. You're fine now.''

''That's easy for you to say. I know I've bitten my tongue in two, and I think my neck's most likely broken.''

''I was talking to the horse, Miss Romney.''

''I should have known,'' she answered bitterly.

''If you think you can manage to hang on for a few more seconds, I'll lead this poor beast back and see about your brother.''

''Of course I can hang on.'' Sarah spoke with more bravado than she felt. She then chose to ignore his lordship's derisive snort.

Tids's bay was peacefully cropping grass when the other two riders joined them. The boy had progressed to a sitting position. But he was reluctant to distance himself from terra firma any more than that.

Lord Graymarsh dismounted. He looked at Tids with more disapproval than sympathy. ''Are you all right?'' he barked.

''I g-guess so.''

Thus reassured, Gray turned to help Sarah dismount. She had anticipated him, however, and was determined to prove herself a horsewoman by getting off alone. He was just in time to be in the way when a tangle of boots and skirt and stirrup sent her sprawling. She clutched at him to break her fall, caught him off balance, knocked him off his feet, and landed on top of him. ''Ooff!'' his lordship commented as the wind escaped his lungs.

It was the bedchamber in the Portsmouth inn all over again. Why she found being enfolded in this odious man's arms such a homey sort of feeling was more than Sarah Romney could understand. Nor could she ever hope to anticipate the Graymarsh reaction to such proximity. In one instance, it had turned him lecherous. In this case, furious.

''I don't appreciate your language, sir.'' Despite the fact that her body was plastered on top of his with an intimacy that even her heavy riding clothes could not obscure, her tone was prim. "I am well aware that I'm an actress, therefore not a lady. But since you are supposed to be a gentleman, I find your conduct inexcusable."

Lord Graymarsh looked into the beautiful, censorious eyes just above him, stared at the disapproving mouth, and came within an ace of kissing it. Just in time he recalled the folly of succumbing to his baser instincts. He swore again instead. "Get off me, woman," he commanded.

"You needn't take that tone. I intend to." She struggled upright, leaving Gray feeling far more bereft than he was prepared for or would admit, even to himself.

A natural reaction to this undefined emotion, which had followed hard upon the fear that he'd be too late to prevent the Romneys from breaking their fool necks, was an increase of fury. "What the devil did you two think you were up to?" he demanded as he rose and dusted himself off.

Sarah, who was feeling the Prodigy for broken bones, grew at least as haughty. "We were out for a morning ride. What else would we be 'up to'?"

Tidswell chimed in defensively. "Lord Petherbridge did say we could use his horses anytime we'd a mind to."

"Did his lordship realize that neither one of you had ever been on a horse before?"

"What an absurd notion." Sarah was glad her back was turned. "Whatever gave you the idea we'd never ridden?"

"Perhaps," he replied dryly, "it was Tidswell clinging to his horse like a monkey on a bolting tiger. Or it could have been you flapping along like the wash caught in a high wind." Graymarsh choked suddenly at the recollection.

Sarah spun to face him. "I'm glad you find it so amusing that we were almost killed. And we can hardly be held responsible for the fact that our horses ran away."

"Oh, can you not? I beg to differ. You are right about

one thing, though. The whole thing's not funny. If I hadn't come along—''

''I assume you're waiting for us to thank you. Well, consider it done.''

''I don't want your thanks,'' he said explosively. ''What I would like is an explanation of why two complete novices chose to take out two of the most spirited horses in Petherbridge's stables without letting the groom know you'd never ridden before in your lives. And don't bother denying that fact again. It won't wash with me.''

''I did not expect riding to be so difficult,'' Sarah answered defensively.

''And I didn't expect you to be so calf-witted.''

''Well, it looks easy enough.'' She bristled. ''And we're actors. Imitators by trade. I observed the riders closely yesterday and didn't foresee any problem in simply doing as they did.''

'Of all the daft— Why didn't you just admit you didn't know how to ride? One of the grooms could have instructed you.''

''Because,'' she blazed, ''people of your sort simply assume that everyone knows how. In the same way it's simply assumed that people own their own carriages, and have a house in town, and—and attend Almack's assemblies. When those people''—she gestured in the direction of the hall—''were planning their horseback excursions, it didn't occur to anyone that we mightn't know how to ride. And I—I just didn't want to admit it, that's all.'' She glared at him. ''Do you think you aristocrats are the only ones entitled to their pride?''

''I think I've no intention of getting into a class war with you.''

''You'd better not.'' Tidswell surprised himself by horning in. Graymarsh might be the owner of the marvelous, if waterlogged, means of flight, but blood was thicker than balloon air. "The fact is, Sarah's at least as well born as you are."

"Tidswell!" Sarah gasped in horror while Gray looked rather worse than startled.

"I don't care. It's true. Papa says so. Sarah's only my half sister, you see." The Prodigy's voice filled with pride. "And her father was a lord. So for all we know, he could have been a higher-up kind of lord than you are."

"Tidswell!" Sarah repeated. She was ready to sink with mortification. Graymarsh watched her curiously. "That's nothing but a Banbury tale and you should not repeat it. Besides, my parentage has nothing to say to anything."

"Yes, it does." Her brother stuck to his guns stubbornly. "It must be the reason you wouldn't admit you'd never ridden. At least I know I would have," he added virtuously.

"Well, never mind all that." Graymarsh thought it was time to change the subject. He felt a protective rush of sympathy for Sarah's embarrassment. "You both are about to get your first lesson now."

"Really, my lord, that won't be necessary." Miss Romney was all icy dignity.

"I ain't about to get back up on that vicious monster," her brother declared.

"Oh, yes, you are. It's the first rule of riding. When a horse dumps you, you climb right back on. And, yes, Miss Romney, it is necessary. For one thing, I don't want my uncle's cattle or your lives imperiled."

"Thank you for the order of your concern."

"And for another," he continued as though she'd never spoken, "it's a long way back. All right now. Please bring your famous actor's training into focus and observe. This, Miss and Master Romney, is the proper technique for mounting. Understand? Now then. Try to imitate me exactly."

Chapter Nine

*Lord and Lady Petherbridge's house party was proceed*ing, for the most part, along traditional lines. Breakfast was served at ten, dinner around five, supper at ten-thirty. Between breakfast and changing for dinner the gentlemen went shooting or fishing. They joined the ladies for a walk, on an outing, or in their dressing rooms. They played billiards in the hall. The ladies spent part of the morning in their own dressing rooms or their hostess's, then walked around the lake or garden, watched the gentlemen fishing, or went for a drive to the neighboring village. Occasionally, visitors called. Wet days were largely spent in the library, rummaging among the books, doing needlework, playing anagrams and backgammon, or simply chatting, as their fancy was struck.

There were some variations, however, in the time-honored routine. Before breakfast, Lord Graymarsh and his reluctant pupils met for riding lessons. Then when he had eaten, Tidswell joined, with even greater reluctance, his hostess's class in moral instruction for the children of her tenants.

Tids considered it quite the most tedious hour imaginable and found his ladyship too prosy again by half. He was filled with wonder at the compliance of the other children until he discovered that they welcomed these classes as a respite from their labors.

At first, Tids had been flattered by Lady Petherbridge's attention. He could imagine his father's delight when he learned of it. But gradually the boy began to wonder about her motives and found it more than coincidental that her ladyship chose the works of Hannah More for their spiritual edification. Lady Petterbridge prefaced each selection from *Practical Piety and Christian Morals* by telling them once again how a misguided Miss More had been associated with the wicked stage, had, in fact, had a flourishing career as a writer of tragedies, but had seen the error of her ways and turned her pen away from the theater toward higher things. The inference was plain. If Miss More could redirect her life, well, so could Master Romney.

"What would Miss More say about your theatricals?" Tids was bold enough to point out some discrepancy in Lady Petherbridge's preaching and her practice.

"There is a world of difference between ladies and gentlemen reading uplifting material for private amusement in their own houses and actors giving sordid performances for hire," was the haughty, less-than-satisfactory reply.

Tids was not the only one puzzled by Lady Petherbridge's choice of entertainment for her guests. Sarah confided her confusion privately to Randolph when the two of them arrived onstage early for the first rehearsal.

She had not yet recovered from the shock of seeing the hall theater. It far eclipsed in grandeur, if not size, any of the provincial playhouses she'd appeared in. The decor was a riot of gilt paint. Golden cupids were in large supply. Ornate plasterwork was rampant. Sconces and chandeliers gleamed with gold and crystal. Miss Romney ran an expert eye around the house. From pit to balcony, she estimated that the theater could seat almost two hundred. She voiced her concern obliquely. "When Lady Petherbridge engaged me to organize her theatricals, I really expected a much larger house party than this one."

"Did you?" Randolph said uneasily.

"Well, yes. It is a bit unusual for the cast to outnumber the audience, don't you think?" (Actually, in the Romney Company experience, it was not really all that rare.)

"Oh, well." Randolph dismissed such trifles carelessly. "As for that, if we come up to snuff in our performance, I expect my aunt will provide us with an audience. Be a good chance for her to have the county in. Noblesse oblige and all that, don't you know."

Sarah did not know. But if Lady Petherbridge's own nephew was not concerned about the oddness of the engagement, well, then, she needn't be. "Oh, there's no question that our performance will come up to snuff," she remarked with a bravado worthy of Adolphus Romney.

The young director had many occasions to eat those words. The first came about half an hour later when the rest of the young people were assembled upon the stage and she attempted to assign the parts.

Sarah had devoted much time and effort in choosing the right vehicle for these amateurs. She had decided upon *The Gamester.* The play had several qualities to recommend it. For one thing, it was written in prose, not verse, and would be less difficult for nonprofessionals to tackle. But more important, the cast of characters exactly fit, in numbers, anyhow, her little group of players.

Before assigning the parts, Sarah outlined the plot. This proved no small task, for the play was complicated, not to mention convoluted. "The male lead, Beverley," she explained, "is a gamester who squanders his own fortune then sells his wife's jewels. He's led astray by a false friend named Stukeley, who is scheming to win Mrs. Beverley for himself. Mr. Lewison, who is in love with the gamester's sister, discovers Stukeley's villainy. Stukeley tries to murder him. In the meantime, Beverley, who has been languishing in debtors' prison, takes poison in despair, then discovers too late that he's inherited another fortune. Mrs. Beverley dies soon afterward of a broken heart."

"My God," Gray was heard to groan underneath his breath.

Given the limitations of her group, Sarah was satisfied that she'd done an excellent job of casting. Mr. Langford's exceptional good looks made him a natural choice for Beverley, the male lead. For the same reason, but with less conviction, she'd given the part of Mrs. Beverley to Miss Crome. She had not hesitated a moment over the villain's role. Lord Graymarsh would do the part of Stukeley. That left the virtuous Lewison to be played by Mr. Milbanke. She herself, in addition to directing, would be obliged to take the minor role of the gamester's sister.

Sarah had not anticipated the amateurs' reactions. Her cast assignments met with instant opposition. Miss Crome, apprehensive of participating in the theatricals at all, had grown quite pale when given the lead role. She asked in a trembling voice to be excused. After Sarah's attempts to persuade her to at least read through the part had failed and Randolph's entreaties hadn't moved her, the Prodigy offered his opinion, with more truth than tact, that anybody who looked like Miss Crome could make a complete cake out of herself onstage and nobody would even notice. But on this issue the pliant Miss Crome proved intractable. Sarah finally offered to exchange parts with her if she would not abandon the project altogether.

That crisis settled, the director hit another snag. Lord

Graymarsh declared that he'd no intention of being involved in such a piece of flummery. He'd work backstage if necessary, but he was damned if he'd play that sapskulled part.

"What's the matter, Gray?" his cousin twitted. "Nose out of joint? Want to be the hero?"

"Not at all. Getting to do you the dirty is the only appealing aspect of the whole silly plot." It was his lordship's considered opinion that the villain Stukeley was *The Gamester's* choicest role. "Which is about like saying you'd prefer the pox to leprosy." And all his brother's wheedling could not induce Graymarsh to change his mind. As for Sarah, she refused even to try, but turned in desperation instead to her brother. "Tids?" she pleaded.

His face was set stubbornly. "You promised I wouldn't have to take a part. I'm stage manager."

"I know I promised. But I did not think to be short one male." The speaking look she shot Graymarsh failed to disconcert him. Nor did her pleading budge her little brother.

"Perhaps if Mr. Milbanke would play Stukeley, you could have the smaller part."

"No! You promised!" But then a look of cunning crept into the Prodigy's eyes. "Of course if you was to do me a favor, I might do you one."

"And what would that favor be?"

"Let me go up in his lordship's balloon."

"No!" There was a long pause while the two Romneys glared at each other. Then Sarah closed her script dramatically. "We'll just have to choose another play, that's all."

"Oh, what the devil. I'll do it." Lord Graymarsh suddenly capitulated with great martyrdom and little grace. "Only how about trading parts with me, Randolph? You did say the part of—who was it, Lewison?—was smaller, didn't you, Miss Romney?"

Sarah nodded, relieved but at the same time feeling things slipping out of her control.

"So, little brother, wouldn't you like a juicier role?"

"But Gray," Gerard protested with a mocking smile, "that's no good. No one will take Randolph seriously as a villain."

"Whereas they would me? Thank you, Coz. What do you say, Miss Romney? The part of Lewison would give me more time to help the Prodigy backstage."

"Very well, then," Sarah grudgingly agreed. She suspected that all this maneuvering was designed to avoid playing romantic scenes with her. Or perhaps he merely wished to place himself opposite Miss Crome. Well, if he had but noticed, her original casting had served both those ends. She pulled herself together and attempted to regain the reins of this runaway rehearsal. But the initial read-through left her even more discouraged and depressed.

Nor did subsequent evening practice sessions serve to lift her spirits. She blamed herself for the lack of progress they were making. As a theater professional, she should, she felt, be able to surmount enough of their difficulties to bring about a creditable performance of *The Gamester*.

The problem was, she could find no similarity between the production of social theatricals and the serious pursuit of earning one's bread and butter. It wasn't that she aimed so high. Heaven knows, the Romney Company had dealt with its own share of miscasting. But never had she had to cope with a character who quailed and quaked as Miss Crome did. And Randolph, though more courageous, was just as hopeless in his role. As for his recalcitrant lordship, any hopes she'd had that he might pick up a bit of zeal for acting faded after one or two rehearsals. Boredom was Lord Graymarsh's overriding emotion. It set the key for his so-called performance.

If there was any bright spot where Graymarsh was concerned, and Sarah tried her best to view it so, it was that his boredom evaporated when Tids introduced him to life behind the scenes. Here Gray's bent for invention ran such riot that the director felt compelled to launch a protest, "All these scenic effects will upstage the drama."

"Good. So much the better for the audience," the nobleman–stage apprentice replied as he and the Prodigy went on to plot a regular orgy of thunder, lightning, hail, fog, wind, and rain.

Mr. Gerard Langford, however, proved the outstanding exception to the general ineptitude. He had, in fact, turned out to be a genuine dramatic find. Well aware of the Corinthian's striking good looks and supreme self-confidence, Sarah had expected a certain aptitude for acting on his part. She had not expected such extraordinary talent. Had Mr. Langford been less well born, Sarah soon decided, the Garricks, Kembles, and Keans of the professional theater might well have had a strong contender for their laurels.

But what was undoubtedly the production's biggest asset also had its down side, the director soon discovered. It was bad enough that Gerard completely overshadowed his fellow amateurs' performances; what was worse was that Sarah was obliged to push her own talents to the limit to reach his level. And she blamed Lord Graymarsh for the fact that she found this so difficult to do. It was humiliating when she, a consummate professional, was reduced to a self-conscious parroter of lines merely because his lordship, hammer in hand, was watching from the wings. And at no point was her craft put more to the test than when the script called for a passionate embrace between the gamester and his wife.

Wearing her director's hat, Sarah had explained how the love scene should be played. Mr. Langford should take her into his arms, then bend her body away from the audience so that the back of his head obscured her face. Thus they would give the illusion of a long and ardent kiss, whereas in reality their lips would never meet.

"Nonsense," said Mr. Langford as he enfolded her in his arms. "Here's how I envision this particular scene." His lips met hers just in time to shut off her protest. Not only did the leading man actually kiss the leading lady, but he continued the intimacy well beyond the scene's requirements, not to mention the bounds of all propriety. Nor did it help matters at all that when Sarah emerged, red of face and gasping, from this expert, unsettling, unprofessional embrace, the first thing she saw was Graymarsh's level, censorious stare.

An unexpected side effect of Mr. Langford's excellence was that it spurred his cousin Randolph on to greater effort. Mr. Milbanke seemed to grow painfully aware of his own inadequacies and pressed his director for private coaching sessions. Sarah soon found this rather wearing, especially since he, like his cousin, seemed to place far too much emphasis on his love scenes at the expense of the rest of his appearances. So she was guiltily grateful—for Randolph's acting needed all the help that she could give it—when at the end of a particularly trying group rehearsal, Mr. Langford took his cousin firmly by the arm. "No private session tonight, cub. Miss Romney needs a rest. And I need you for billiards."

Sarah took full advantage of her reprieve and went immediately to bed. But after a full hour spent tossing and turning in the unsuccessful endeavor to find a comfortable position, she finally abandoned the notion of sleep and lit her bedside candle. Reading would rid her mind of its disconcerting tendency to dwell upon a particular, odious member of the aristocracy. She picked up the three leather-bound volumes stacked on the bedside table and examined each in turn. They proved to be a weighty collection of sermons, the inevitable copy of Hannah More, and *The Mysteries of Udolpho.* The last, Sarah surmised, must have been left by some former guest. It hardly seemed to reflect the literary taste of Lady Petherbridge. She decided to read it. Though possibly less soporific than the other two, at least the Gothic novel would keep her mind from dwelling upon a certain incident in a Portsmouth inn and the feel of a bare chest, strong arms, demanding mouth . . . Resolutely, she opened the work of Mrs. Radcliffe.

The cure proved worse than the disease. Sarah did forget all about Lord Graymarsh, but she became so obsessed with the possibility of clanking chains and fearsome cries and moaning specters that she raised her eyes from the printed page every few seconds to peer around her, trying to penetrate the deep shadows that lay beyond the small pool of candlelight. The room that by daylight seemed so welcoming had suddenly turned sinister. The dark mass that once had been a wardrobe appeared ominous, undefined. Surely it had moved! Was creeping toward her! And was that a bulge behind the damask drapery? Could something inhuman, unthinkable, be lurking there, choosing its time to pounce?

Don't be ridiculous. You're letting your imagination get out of hand. Sarah gave herself a mental dressing-down. What you need is rest. Blow out your candle and go to sleep! So screwing her courage to the sticking point, she inhaled a deep breath, then watched the yellow candle flame bend and elongate, sputter, and go out. And at the precise moment of total darkness, she realized three things: she had heard an ominous, prolonged creaking; she was not alone; and she had not exhaled her breath. She took care of the omission immediately in a long, bloodcurdling scream.

The Honorable Randolph Milbanke had not wished to advertise his presence to anyone else who might be abroad in Pether Hall. So he had made his way down the corridor without benefit of candle, relying on the faint moonlight drifting through the open window at its end. Not being a disciple of Mrs. Radcliffe, he took no notice of the slight breeze that fanned his carefully styled hair. What he did observe was a trickle of light beneath Miss Romney's door. The actress, he deduced, was still awake. The gentlemanly thing would be, of course, to knock. But prudence and the proximity of other houseguests demanded a different course. Randolph turned the doorknob very slowly, trying to reduce its tendency to squeak. He eased the door ajar, thereby creating the fatal draft that snuffed Miss Romney's candle.

Her piercing shriek caused him to drop the tray he bore. The ensuing clang and clatter, combined with a sharp, crashing, splintering sound, compounded Miss Romney's terror and increased the volume of her screams.

Instinctively, Randolph sprang toward the bed. His one thought was to persuade its occupant to cut the caterwauling before she waked the dead. The maneuver was to prove a grave mistake. Unlike the Gothic heroines she admired, Miss Romney was not prone to swoon in a crisis. Instead, as the dark form lunged her way, she snatched the heavy brass candlestick from its stand and swung it with all her might. The blow was glancing, but if sufficed. It sideswiped Randolph's nose, which immediately gushed blood. His howl of pain now merged with Miss Romney's shrieks of fear.

"Sarah! My God, Sarah! What's happening!"

Lord Graymarsh had been awakened from a deep sleep to dash groggily toward the outcry. It was plain good luck and not acuity that caused his bare feet to spring safely over two shattered crystal goblets as he honed in on the dim figure attacking the damsel on the bed. In actuality, Randolph had just succeeded in clapping his hand over Miss Romney's mouth and was trying to explain his presence the best he could when a pair of rough hands jerked him backward off the bed. A source of light miraculously materialized and shone on a familiar gold brocade dressing gown. "Damn you, Gerry," his lordship croaked, "this time you've gone too far!" Gray swung the midnight marauder around and delivered a right cross to the jaw before he realized his mistake. Randolph groaned, his legs buckled, and he sank limply to the floor.

"I do think you owe me an apology, Gray, old fellow." Mr. Langford held his candle aloft and looked down at the stricken Randolph. "And did you have to bloody the poor idiot's nose? He's bled all over my best dressing gown."

"He didn't bloody my dose." Randolph thickly set the record straight. "Miss Romney took care of dat. Gray merely broke my jaw."

Lord Graymarsh glared at his brother with less pity than distaste. "It's more than you deserve. What the devil were you up to?"

"Don't be obtuse." Mr. Langford's eyes wandered from his pilfered dressing gown to the broken goblets; to the wine bottle, mercifully still intact, that had rolled in the direction of the wardrobe; and finally came to rest on Miss Romney, who was sitting upright amid the tumbled bedclothes and trying to adjust her ruffled nightcap and regain her poise. The latter endeavor was not aided by the fact that her two gallant rescuers were clad only in their nightshirts. "I'm afraid, Graymarsh, it's all too obvious what your brother was up to." Mr. Langford clucked his disapproval.

"I just wanted Miss Romney to help me with my lines, that's all," the guilty party muttered. And three pairs of eyes took due note of the well-worn copy of *The Gamester* resting not far from the dented tray.

"There's a theater for that sort of thing." Lord Graymarsh sounded dangerous. "Are you all right, Miss Romney? Did he hurt you?"

"Did *I* hurt *her*?" Randolph's sense of injury was mounting. What he'd envisioned as a romantic interlude had become a classic nightmare. "She damned near killed me. I never laid a hand on her except to try to stop her screeching before she roused the household. Which I obviously did not succeed in.'' He eyed his kin with loathing.

''Oh, my goodness!'' Sarah suddenly awoke to the fact that, horrifying as this imbroglio was, it had the potential to become far worse. ''Do you think the others heard?''

''I doubt it,'' Gerard reassured her. ''If they had, they'd be here by now. The Stanhopes across the hall are as deaf as posts. The Prodigy's next door? Well, then, I assume he's dead.''

''Oh, Tidswell can sleep through anything.''

''Evidently. So, except for us, everyone else is in the east wing. Let's trust that even your professional projection can't carry quite that far.''

''You know, Miss Romney, it really wasn't necessary to go screeching like a banshee and then nearly kill me with your candlestick.'' Randolph felt his nose gingerly and eyed her with reproach. ''If you didn't want me here, all you had to do was say so. I'd have left. A gentleman, don't you know.''

''That, dear brother, is open to question.'' Graymarsh pulled him to his feet. ''Apologize to Miss Romney, and let's leave her in peace.''

''I won't apologize for what I'd no intention of ever doing.'' Randolph set his swelling jaw stubbornly, then winced. ''You and Gerry ought to know I'd never attack Miss Romney, even if she does seem to think I would.''

Sarah suddenly felt sorry for young Randolph. At best, he was quite unsuited for the Don Juan role he'd tried to play. And to be so humiliated before his more sophisticated relatives must be far worse punishment than his bloodied nose and battered jaw. Now that she'd recovered from her fright, Sarah felt more than a bit embarrassed herself that she'd not handled the incident with more aplomb. Under ordinary circumstances, she might have sent the callow youth off with a flea in his ear but with his dignity more or less intact. She tried now to smooth things over for him a bit.

"Though it was inexcusable for you to invade my privacy, Mr. Milbanke, I am sorry that I screamed and hit you. I would not have done so had I realized just what, er, who you were. But the fact is . . ." She was bogged down in a fresh rush of embarrassment as the truth of what she'd actually supposed came home to her.

"Yes, Miss Romney, you were saying?" Lord Graymarsh prodded politely as her silence lengthened.

"I lost my train of thought," she mumbled, while Mr. Langford, who'd been looking puzzled, drew near and held his candle over the open volume beside her. He gave a wicked chuckle. His cousins looked offended by such misplaced mirth. Miss Romney's mortification mounted. "*The Mysteries of Udolpho!* You were reading this, Miss Romney, when my cousin came creeping in?" She nodded, and he laughed again. "Well, that does explain a lot. Poor Randolph. What abysmal timing! May I suggest, Miss Romney, that you place a chair underneath the doorknob after we are gone and confine your future reading to Hannah More? Come, gentlemen."

He moved to the door and opened it the merest crack to assure that the coast was clear. The three young men eased out into the hall, two of them ghostly specters in their bedclothes, the other a fallen angel in bloodstained gold. Gerard lighted the threesome down the hall. "You owe me a dressing gown, Randolph." He spoke in an undertone. "And if you'd bothered to ask my permission before you took it, I could have saved you some pain with a bit of free advice. Never pay clandestine, nocturnal visits to Gothic novel readers. Scaring a lady out of her wits is no fit prelude to seduction." Graymarsh shook suddenly with laughter, and his brother gave him a dirty look.

"Still," Gerald continued thoughtfully, "I should be grateful you didn't ask. My conscience would have been sorely tried. As it is, I didn't have to feel obligated to try to stop you from ruining your chances with Miss Romney. On further consideration, you needn't bother to replace my robe. A dressing gown is a small price to pay for a rival's elimination. Uncle's fortune should buy no end of gold brocade. Sleep tight, Cousin Randolph. Sweet dreams."

"Go to hell, Gerry." As he stepped inside his threshold, Randolph blew his cousin's candle out. "You go there, too, Gray." He directed this remark toward more smothered laughter in the darkness just before he slammed his chamber door.

Chapter Ten

"*Hurry up, will you, Sarah!*"

Miss Romney gave her brother a jaundiced look. He had no right to appear well rested. Or so eager. She settled the tall riding hat on her chestnut curls and pinched her cheeks to restore a little color. Satisfied that they now harmonized with her bloodshot eyes, she sighed and turned from the cheval glass. "I thought you hated riding." It had been true. Tids was used to approach his horse like a Montague eyeing a Capulet.

"Where'd you ever get such a maggoty notion? I like it above all things."

"That's not what you used to say." She reluctantly followed him out of her chamber door. "You used to say that you wanted no part of anything that has a leg fastened on each of its four corners."

"That was before I became such a bang-up rider."

It was true. Tids had made amazing progress. He was, of course, an athlete whose natural abilities had been increased by all the tumbling, swordplay, and dancing he'd mastered for the stage. Still, Sarah conceded mentally as they made their way down the azalea-lined walkway toward the stables, much of the credit had to be given to his instructor. Not only was Lord Graymarsh an accomplished horseman—a nonpareil, in fact—he had approached his tutorial task with amazing tact and patience. Insofar as the Prodigy was concerned, at least.

Tids paused at a turn in the path to allow Sarah to catch up. "What's wrong with you this morning, anyhow? You're slower than treacle and crosser than anything." He peered up at her puffy eyes and haggard face. "What's more you look like the very deuce," he added clinically.

"Thank you. I did not get a whole lot of sleep last night."

"Didn't you?" He seemed interested. "Come to think on it, I didn't rest too well myself. Kept dreaming there was a regular rumpus going on. People up and down the hall. Doors slamming. Somebody screeching. Maybe it wasn't just a dream. Did you hear anything?"

"No. That is, well, I'm not really sure. Perhaps I did hear something. Do you have to walk so fast?"

"Don't be such a grouch. Don't you want to ride?"

Sarah did not. At least she did not want to ride with Graymarsh. Or even to see him, when it came to that. She'd been tempted to flee Pether Hall altogether rather than face any of the trio who'd come barging into her room the night before. Only the thought of facing Adolphus Romney had kept her there.

As they passed through the stable-yard gate, Sarah's faint hope flickered and went out. She'd clung to the notion that Graymarsh wouldn't appear. He'd naturally oversleep. Or he'd feel too awkward after last night's fiasco to want to confront her. But there he was, dressed in an impeccable dark-blue riding coat, rested and unflustered, leading a small, spirited chestnut around and around in the yard. From the cool, impersonal glance he gave her as they approached, no one would ever have suspected he'd come rushing into her bedchamber, barefoot and in his nightshirt, in the dead of night.

"Oh, I say! Is that for me?" Tids's eyes glowed as he ran toward the baron and the chestnut.

"Whoa there. Steady now." Gray spoke as much to the boy as to the horse. He relinquished the bridle to the Prodigy. "Walk him a bit. Get acquainted. I suppose you brought some sugar along? Yes, of course."

"Ooooh, he's beautiful," Tids breathed. "I can't believe I'm actually going to ride him. He really is a prime bit of blood." The Prodigy was so taken with the phrase that he repeated it. "A prime bit of blood if I ever saw it."

"Well, I do think you're ready to graduate from the hack that you've been using."

From Gray's disparaging tone, no one would have suspected that he himself had personally chosen the hack for Tids. After the Romneys' first disastrous ride, he had given the poor stable boy a solid dressing-down for not recognizing "complete flats" when he saw them and had ordered him to saddle the two most plodding, docile animals in his uncle's stables. Now the same mare, the actress noted, was once more saddled and stood waiting for her. She felt her resentment surge. Her progress had been every bit as good as Tids. But trust his nibs to ignore that fact.

As Tidswell eagerly scrambled onto the chestnut's back, Gray strolled over to help Sarah mount. "Don't bother," she said waspishly. "The poor thing needs to lie down, anyhow. Then I can merely step on."

"Nose out of joint?" He grinned suddenly and then helped her into the saddle. "I could order you another horse, of course, but I thought you might be a bit fatigued this morning."

"Lord Graymarsh, if you dare to refer to last night's odious affair, I shall endeavor to have this ancient nag collapse on top of you."

"Last night? Now why would I mention last night? Actually, I had planned to discuss literature. Have you read any interesting books lately that you'd care to recommend?" His face was tightly controlled, but he couldn't subdue, nor could she miss, the laughter in his eyes. Sarah dug her heels into her horse's flanks. The ill-favored equine gave the world an injured look and plodded off in the direction the galloping chestnut had taken.

Lord Graymarsh maintained a sedate pace by Sarah's side, though it was obvious that his mount was chafing at the bit. They rode in silence for a while. "Lovely morning," he finally observed.

"I think it looks like rain."

"Well, yes. Bright sunshine. Cloudless sky. Bad signs, those."

"I was referring to the breeze. It has a decided dampness. And the sky's not cloudless."

He rose in the stirrups to squint with intense exaggeration down the meadow they were crossing and up above a tree-crowned hill where one tiny puff-of-cotton cloud was seen to float. "You're right. I stand corrected. It does look ominous."

She giggled then, and he sighed with relief. "Thank God. I was beginning to think you'd lost your sense of humor."

Sarah reverted to her scowl. "I assure you, sir, my sense of humor is quite intact. It has simply found no cause for amusement in any of the happenings of late."

"None at all?"

"None." She firmly closed that subject. Then after a

lengthy silence, she broached another. "What I do not understand at all is why I was asked here."

The question had an odd effect. For a moment, Graymarsh actually looked startled. But he reined in his horse just then to allow her to precede him through a narrow opening in the hedgerow they'd been following, and by the time he drew abreast again, his face was quite composed. "Surely there's no secret about why my aunt asked you. She wished to amuse her guests. Theatricals are quite the thing at country houses. They help break the tedium."

"Not here they don't. In the first place, there aren't enough people to justify the endeavor."

"I beg to differ. A larger group might not so soon grow sick of one another."

"And in the second place," she continued, ignoring the implication, "there's little interest in dramatics. Poor Miss Crome is absolutely terrified at the thought of performing. And you would prefer being stretched out on the rack."

He laughed. "Oh, that's coming it a bit strong. I'll admit I haven't any desire to disport myself for public amusement, but you have to admit my scenic effects are rather good."

"Rather good? Oh, you are far too modest, my lord. Your fog is spectacular. It will no doubt obscure the entire second act, and"—she held up a restraining hand—"before you tell me that could be a merciful occurrence, let me just say that I'm well aware of it."

"You wrong me." He grinned, reminding her suddenly of why she'd initially found him so attractive. "I wasn't about to make such an ungentlemanly remark. Besides"—he grew serious once again—"it would have been untrue. You and Gerry are very good together."

"Mr. Langford does show an amazing ability as an actor."

"I find nothing amazing about it. Gerry has been acting

all his life.'' He paused deliberately. ''He is especially skilled when it comes to love scenes.''

''I beg to differ. I think Mr. Langford and I do deal well together onstage for the most part. Where our performance breaks down, though, is in the love scenes.'' She was attempting to sound professional and detached but was actually feeling quite uncomfortable. ''Mr. Langford, as I've tried to point out to him, quite fails to maintain the proper esthetic distance.''

''That's one way to put it. Another is that he acts like a whoremonger.''

Sarah's embarrassment was replaced by anger. ''Your lordship certainly has a way with words. But never mind. I'll accept your delicate turn of phrase—which you would never dream of employing in Miss Crome's presence, by the by. But I am, after all, an actress. Yes, Mr. Langford does use the excuse of the play's stage directions to take certain liberties. Your brother, it seems, needs no excuse to treat me like a cyprian. And we both know that I have you to thank for their attitude.''

''Me to thank?'' He looked astonished. ''I assure you, Miss Romney, I've no notion of what you're talking about.''

''Oh, have you not? Well, perhaps I do overstate the case a bit when I blame you entirely for the liberties the others take. Like you, they simply make certain assumptions about actresses. We are all women of easy virtue and''—her tone was bitter—''fair game. Especially for the gentry. But I do think Mr. Langford's attitude is rather more understandable than yours was. He did, after all, find the two of us in a most compromising situation.''

''That has nothing to say to Gerry's behavior. I'm sure he—''

''Of course it has,'' she interrupted. ''And I've no doubt that he told your brother of it. The fact that Mr. Langford caught us—well, you know how,'' she said, coloring, "simply reinforced the general belief that *actress* and *lightskirt* are interchangeable designations. But since I do not require the good opinion of any of you *gentlemen*"—she placed undue stress upon the term—"I will not waste my breath in trying to convince you that you're wrong."

"You are bitter, aren't you?"

"Bitter? That three gentlemen of the ton should try to give me a slip on the shoulder? La, sir," she mocked him, "I'm that honored I'm fair beside myself."

"You're wrong, you know." He held a tight rein on both his horse and temper. "Never mind Gerry and me for the moment. Let's talk about last night. No, I insist." He waved away her protest. "That's what's put you up on your high ropes, isn't it? My brother was stupid, gauche. He behaved abominably. But he was not trying to give you a slip on the shoulder, I assure you."

"Fustian. Why else would he pursue me? Or why would Mr. Langford? But to set the record straight, I no longer count you as a potential seducer."

"Thank you. I'm glad to see your estimate of my character rise."

"On the contrary, it hasn't. I merely think that there's nothing like being made to feel ridiculous—as when Mr. Langford interrupted our little bedroom farce in Portsmouth—to cool the passions. For the same reason, I don't expect to be pursued by Mr. Milbanke any longer. But to be quite honest," she admitted with sudden candor, "I don't think you were ever all that eager. I believe you merely thought you were obliging me. And I must admit, if one ignores the fact that I stumbled over your boots, as you seemed determined to overlook, it must have appeared that I was flinging myself at you. Especially since, according to your cousin, you take pursuit for granted."

"Gerry said that, did he?"

"Oh, yes. He insisted on walking me home from the inn that day and made all sorts of excuses for your behavior.

It seems you are rich as Croesus and, consequently, the constant prey of fortune hunters of all descriptions. Some with matrimony in mind. Others—and I'm sure you placed me in this category—more than willing to settle for a carte blanche."

From the grim set of Gray's mouth, Sarah had the satisfaction of concluding that she'd touched him on the raw.

"As I noted," he shot back, "you do sound bitter. And, if I may say so, quick to misinterpret the attentions of gentlemen. Perhaps your own . . . obscure parentage has made you too suspicious. No, before you fly off into the boughs again, I'm not referring now to my ill-advised attempts at lovemaking in Portsmouth. To set the record straight, I do regret that. And beg pardon for it. If I have an excuse, it's that I'm not nearly so widely pursued as my cousin intimated. In fact, he painted a rather distorted picture. You see, it was an entirely new experience for me to find an unaccompanied young lady in my room. That—pray forgive me, Miss Romney—is more the behavior of women of another stamp."

"Oh, I'm quite aware of that now. And it's useless to say that I intended to see you in the public parlor. And that I was merely concerned for the burns you had suffered. You will not believe it, and I do not need your good opinion. But I would like to clear up one point you tried to make. I am not bitter about my parentage."

"Oh, no?"

"No. I have never had any reason to be other than proud of it. My stepfather is kind and affectionate. He saw to it that I received an education he could ill afford. Most important, he has schooled me in a profession that I take great pride in—in spite of its occupational hazards, such as loss of reputation."

"But Tidswell said your father—"

"Was a nobleman? That's moonshine."

"Very well, then. That wrecks my explanation for your

bitterness. And explodes my theory that would account for your prejudice against gentlemen. Oh, yes, don't deny it. You've made heavy weather about how all actresses are tarred with the same brush because a few are no better than the cyprian sisterhood. But aren't you just as hard on gentlemen who dangle after actresses? Do their motives always have to be suspect? All right, then, I've already pleaded guilty to misconduct in the Royal Hart. As for Gerard, you'd do well to be warned against him. He's at least the libertine he'd have you believe that I am. But I do take exception to your views on Randolph—in spite of last night's escapade. Undoubtedly he's pursuing you. But there's no reason for you to conclude that his motives are dishonorable."

"That, begging your lordship's pardon, is the biggest pack of nonsense I've ever heard. Of course his motives are dishonorable. Honorable would imply intent to wed. And for a gentleman of your class to pursue me with a view toward marriage—well, I'd either have to be another Helen of Troy, which my looking glass denies, or be possessed of a fortune to rival yours. So I don't think your younger brother is quite the innocent you take him for. What do you say to that?"

"Perhaps you'd better get another looking glass."

Unfortunately, the Prodigy came galloping back just then to ride beside them and expound at length on the remarkable merits of his horse before Sarah could collect herself enough to ask just what on earth his lordship had meant by such an odd reply.

Chapter Eleven

"*Augusta Petherbridge's eccentricity is well known* and accepted. But I do think that in this case she has gone far beyond the bounds of what is proper." Lady Emma Crome did not have to rearrange her facial muscles much to show disapproval. That was their natural set. Even so, there was a subtle alteration of expression that caused her daughter to brace herself for what was to follow.

It was midmorning, and her ladyship had seized the chance to get her daughter alone on the pretext that they should jointly pen a letter to Mr. Crome. Evelina had dutifully seated herself at the rosewood writing table in her mother's bedchamber, only to find that correspondence was not uppermost on Lady Emma's mind.

Her parent found it helpful to pace about the room as she unleashed her feelings. The chamber assigned to her, which had been recently and cheerfully redecorated in the Chinese fashion, seemed an inappropriate setting both for Lady Emma and her lecture. "As much as it pains me to say so," she continued, "as much as it goes against the grain with me to criticize a personage of Lady Petherbridge's social standing—for think what you will of her, Evelina, her antecedents are above reproach. The Milbankes are one of England's oldest, most distinguished families, a fact I cannot stress too often in your hearing, daughter. But while it is true that rank carries with it privilege, and we can, therefore, forgive some degree of eccentricity in those well born—the Regent's conduct, for example, would never be tolerated in a personage of lesser degree—I do believe that in the case of this house party Augusta Petherbridge has gone well beyond eccentricity." Lady Emma paused dramatically. "She has reached impropriety."

"I don't quite understand," her daughter ventured.

"I know that you do not understand, Evelina. You are far too young, too unworldly to understand. You must simply take my word that it is not at all the thing—and an insult, however unwitting, to you, my dear—to have that actress person as the only other young lady—no, I will not use that term—the only other young *female* present. And to treat a person of her station as a guest! It really is too much to countenance! Lady Petherbridge, in my opinion, has a great deal to answer for."

"But I like Miss Romney." Indeed, no greater proof of that regard could have been offered than that Miss Crome dared to voice an opinion counter to her parent's. "And her manners are quite proper. Really, if it were not for the theatricals"—the very term made Evelina shudder—"one would never suspect she was on the stage. And she truly is amusing. She says the most diverting things." Evelina giggled at the memory. "S-she called Lord Graymarsh a villain! Not an ordinary one, mind you. She had all sorts of descriptions to go with it. I never was quite so diverted, I declare.''

''Well, I must say!'' Lady Emma stopped her pacing to glare at her daughter. ''I am shocked that you, Evelina, should be amused by such rag-mannered outbursts. I need no better illustration of the point that I strove to make. You should not be required to associate with that type of person. Lord Graymarsh a villain, indeed! I am shocked. The young woman is coarser than I imagined.''

''Actually, I think she was merely quoting something or other. At least that is what Mr. Langford says.'' Miss Crome tried valiantly to champion Sarah, but her defense was weakening. ''The others seem to like her quite well,'' she finished lamely.

''Humph! You are speaking now of young gentlemen, who will always like females of a certain stamp.''

''Oh, I don't believe Miss Romney—''

''Of course she is.'' There was no arguing with Lady Emma in full spate. ''She is an actress, a member of a notorious profession. Why, the stories that circulate about Edmund Kean alone are enough to— But I will not sully your tender ears, Evelina. The point I intend to make is that I wish you to have as little as possible to do with that Romney person.''

''But—'' her daughter began, and was once more interrupted.

''I know. I know. You have been placed in an intolerable situation where she is the only other young woman in the party. It will be impossible to shun her altogether. If only Lady Scriven had come.'' Lady Emma sighed.

''But Mama,'' Evelina protested, ''Lady Scriven's behavior is most improper. She is known to actually do all those things that you only suspect Miss Romney of.''

''Lady Scriven is one of the nobility. She has been married. Two facts that set her above the harsher judgments of society. And while I do not approve of her mode of living and would not under other circumstances consider her a fit companion for a young lady of your tender years and strict upbringing, when I consider her influence in contrast to Miss Romney's, well, I can only repine that she is not among us. Lady Scriven's place in society is unquestioned. She is received everywhere. Whereas only Augusta Petherbridge would permit a third-rate actress to mingle with her guests. Avoid Miss Romney, Evelina,'' her mother ordered.

''That is the first thing I wished to speak of,'' she continued. ''The second is even more vital to your future happiness. And here I must confess that I am not pleased with you, my dear. You have been given a heaven-sent opportunity to fix Lord Graymarsh's interest, and instead of profiting from the intimacy a house party offers, you actually appear to go out of your way to avoid his lordship.''

Evelina picked up the quill pen from the desk and began to run its feather nervously between her fingers. ''But Mama,'' she protested, ''Lord Graymarsh does not appear to have an interest in me to fix.''

''Nonsense.'' Her mother seated herself on the other side of the desk and removed the pen from her daughter's fingers. ''You must learn to value yourself more highly, Evelina dear. Lady Petherbridge and I have only recently discussed this very subject. And I will say that Augusta, for all her oddities, is very sensible in these matters. She agrees it's time Graymarsh married. His dear father has been gone for some three years now.'' Lady Emma dabbed her eyes affectingly with a handkerchief despite the fact that her acquaintanceship with the late baron was slight. ''And she thinks that you and he should deal very well together. 'Graymarsh does not care overly much for society and would probably like someone who is quiet' was the way she phrased it. But the thing is, my dear, you must make a greater push to captivate his lordship.''

"But I do not know how to set my cap for a gentleman." Evelina was looking more and more distressed.

Her mother spoke in soothing tones. "I know you do not, my dear. That is why I must contrive to help you."

And not being one to let the grass grow underneath her feet, that very afternoon Lady Emma forged an opportunity to bring her daughter and Lord Graymarsh together.

The day being particularly fine, the entire party had moved outdoors, with the exception of Lady Stanhope who, complaining of the staggers, had dosed herself with calomel and gone to bed. The gentlemen, joined by Lady Petherbridge and Master Tidswell, planned to fish. Miss Crome and Miss Romney elected to sketch.

Miss Romney had gone ahead and was on a grassy rise that afforded a good view of the lake when Miss Crome, under her parent's disapproving eye, actually had the temerity to ask, "May I sit beside you?" Lady Emma was just about to open her pursed mouth and point out that sketching, like fishing, was best done in solitude and suggest that Evelina find another location, when Lord Graymarsh, after rejecting several other spots, decided to wet his line in Miss Romney's vicinity. Mr. Langford, who had had the same idea, gave him a speaking look and moved on past. Randolph, coloring at the sight of Sarah, seemed relieved when Lady Petherbridge commandeered him to bait her hook. They and the other anglers spaced themselves around the lake.

The good tactician must be flexible. Lady Emma revised her plans. Rather than remove her daughter from a strategic location so near Lord Graymarsh, her ladyship decided to shift Sarah instead. "My dear Miss Romney," she remarked as she spread her handkerchief, inadequate for her designs, upon the grass and lowered her ample posterior onto it, "I do believe your brother requires your assistance."

Sarah glanced down the lakeshore where Tidswell did

have his line tangled and was struggling with it. "Oh, I'm sure he will manage," she said carelessly.

"He seems rather young to be left unattended. Do you not agree?'

"Tidswell? He's twelve." Sarah was not slow to comprehend the motive behind her ladyship's maneuvering and was amused. She was determined to hold her ground.

"I myself would never dream of leaving a small child alone so near the water." After delivering this setdown, Lady Emma lapsed into icy silence that lasted only until Lord Graymarsh, moments later, hooked a fish.

"Oh, Evelina!" She was in transports. "His lordship has caught a fish! Isn't it thrilling? Do go see!"

"Mama, please!" Miss Crome whispered in an agony of embarrassment.

"Come, Evelina. You are longing, I know, to see it. We must observe how he removes it from the hook." She lumbered to her feet, then thrust out a commanding hand to help her daughter up. "I'm sure Lord Graymarsh deserves our admiration for his sporting feat."

"Will you not come, too, Miss Romney?" Misery cried out for company.

"No, thank you," Sarah replied politely. "The excitement might prove more than I could stand." Then aware that none of their conversation had escaped his lordship, she added mischievously, "But I do agree wholeheartedly with your mother. That fish should be seen at close range. Its size prohibits any more distant admiration."

Gray had just enough time to stare at Sarah in a manner meant to be repressive, but which, in spite of himself, evolved into a broad grin before he was beset by Lady Emma and a mortified Evelina.

After the fish had been exclaimed over, nothing would do but that Lord Graymarsh should share his singular skill. "My daughter has been yearning to learn to fish for the longest time. Have you not, Evelina dear?"

Sarah did manage to choke off a giggle as the red-faced Miss Crome stammered, "Oh, yes. For ages." But when Lord Graymarsh, proffering a worm, asked solemnly, "Would you like to bait the hook?" and Evelina shrieked and backed away, a fit of coughing was the only outlet she could find to offset a burst of laughter.

Ashamed of his mischievous impulse and amazed that he was at the same time longing to laugh with Sarah over it, Gray obligingly baited the hook and handed the fishing pole to Miss Crome with a few instructions on what to do if she felt a nibble. The poor girl looked so mortified that Graymarsh took pity on her. He did his best to set her at ease, chatting easily and at length about the choice fishing sites in the county, as though believing that Miss Crome really had developed a consuming passion for the sport.

Graymarsh actually had a double motive for prosing on about the art of angling. Besides wishing to spare Miss Crome the agonies of upholding her part in a conversation, he hoped to bore her behemoth of a mother into going about her business and leaving them alone. In the first instance he was quite successful. Miss Crome seemed to realize he wished to make her feel at ease and was touchingly grateful for it. But in the latter he was doomed to failure. A powder blast would not have sufficed to remove Lady Emma from Evelina's side. The scheming mama had too little faith in her daughter's powers of entrapment to risk leaving her on her own.

Feeling that the fishing maneuver had been singularly successful, Lady Emma launched a new offensive. "Evelina will give me a scold for saying so, your lordship," she gushed, "for you know how young ladies hate to admit they even think of—let alone discuss—young gentlemen, but my daughter was saying just the other day how much she envies you."

"Indeed? And why do you envy me, Miss Crome?" Gray was immediately sorry for the question when it became evident that the young lady addressed had not the slightest notion of an answer.

"No need to be missish, dear." Lady Emma tried to cover her daughter's bewilderment. "You may just as well admit it. You were envying his lordship's freedom to soar in the air in his magnificent balloon. You were saying that if you were a man you would like ballooning above all things."

Hearing another choking fit from the grassy slope behind them, Gray raised his voice a bit. "How refreshing, Miss Crome, to find a young lady so enthusiastic. It will amaze you to learn, I'm sure, that some females are actually prejudiced against ballooning. Some have the hypocrisy to term it hazardous while at the same time approving of far more dangerous sport. Take fencing as an example. I once knew a female who was knocked flat by a sword—almost decapitated, in fact—but who still thought ballooning suicidal. I find such an attitude incomprehensible."

"Quite absurd." Lady Emma shook her head disdainfully. "But then what could one expect from a female who would actually engage in swordplay?" She seemed to have a strong suspicion of that female's identity. "I can assure you that my daughter would never do anything so vulgar. But I certainly see nothing at all either unladylike or dangerous in a balloon ascension. That is if you, dear Lord Graymarsh, were at the helm, to borrow a nautical figure of speech. I am convinced that Evelina would be perfectly safe with you. Will you not grant her fondest wish and take her up with you?"

There was a gasp. Evelina turned white. Her fishing pole dropped from nerveless fingers. Just as Lord Graymarsh plunged an arm elbow-deep in after it, Miss Crome, uttering a soft moan, crumpled in a heap of blue-sprigged muslin in the green grass at his feet.

The collapse precipitated a rush of activities. Gray consigned his fishing rod to its watery fate and wheeled to help

Miss Crome. Miss Romney dropped her sketchbook and came running down the slope. Equidistant but in opposite directions from the fallen beauty, Tidswell Romney and Gerard Langford abandoned their fishing rods and sprinted toward the scene. The only person who stayed calm was Lady Emma. Annoyance seemed her overriding humor. She pulled a vial of sal volatile from her reticule and held it to her daughter's nose.

Gerard and Tidswell arrived in a dead heat. "Is she d-dead?" the latter said, gasping.

"Don't be ridiculous," Lady Emma snapped. "My daughter has merely swooned."

If the race along the lakeshore had been uncharacteristic of the languid Mr. Langford, the look of concern on his handsome face seemed even more misplaced. As the young lady began to cough and stir, it was relief as much as anger that caused him to turn to his cousin. "What the devil did you say to her to bring this on? Surely you must realize how sensitive Miss Crome is?"

"What did I say? Don't be daft, Gerry. The girl just collapsed. I don't know why."

"Oh, no, you are unjust, Mr. Langford. You must not blame his lordship." Lady Emma seemed much more perturbed over this possibility than over her daughter's condition. "It's the heat, I'm sure. Poor Evelina is so delicate."

"Nonsense!" Sarah was having her own reaction, brought on by fright when Miss Crome fainted, now fueled by guilt. How could she have been amused by a scene that had caused her new friend acute distress! "The heat has nothing to do with any of this. The poor girl's terrified at the prospect of going up in that—that odious balloon. That's why she fainted."

"You're actually proposing to take Miss Crome up in that flying coffin! Damn you, Gray!" Mr. Langford's eyes glittered dangerously. He spoke through tightly clenched, perfect teeth.

Lord Graymarsh looked sufficiently annoyed to welcome a battle. But before he could pick up the challenge, the Prodigy, whose concern for the beauty had evaporated with this new development, chimed in. "You're taking the balloon up again, sir? Oh, when? Please, sir, may I go? Please say yes. I'd be no bother. You'd hardly know I was there."

"Oh, Tids, do be quiet!" his sister commanded.

"I will not! If a mere female like Miss Crome, who's scared of her own shadow, can take a balloon ride, I don't see why you won't let me go. I'm sure Miss Crome would like to have my company. Or, better yet, would let me take her place, for I can't believe she actually wishes to take a balloon ride."

That young lady's lids had fluttered open under her mother's ministrations. She was gazing uncomprehendingly at the many faces staring down at her. But at the sound of the word *balloon*, memory came flooding back. She gave a piteous little moan and swooned again.

"I swear it, Gray," Mr. Langford blazed, "you'll answer to me for this." He then knelt down with a complete disregard for the effects of grass upon biscuit-colored pantaloons. Ignoring the formidable Lady Emma, he picked up the beauty's limp fair hand and began to rub her wrists briskly with strong, slim fingers. "Miss Crome," he murmured softly. "Miss Crome." The eyelids fluttered open once again and fastened on the face behind the soothing voice. "It's all right, Evelina," Mr. Langford continued in the same calming tone. "There's no need to be alarmed. Lord Graymarsh has no intention of taking you up in his balloon. Have you, Gray?" He shot a lethal look up at his cousin.

"No, of course not," the sorely tried aeronaut answered. "And I never have had, as anyone but a gudgeon would realize." The words were intended for his lordship's cousin. And no one but Sarah saw the offended look they brought to Lady Emma's face. Once again the unfortunate actress had to bring all her theatrical training into play to keep from giggling.

"I don't see why everyone is so dead set against balloon rides," the Prodigy muttered. "I'd do it in a minute."

"Miss Crome, do you think you can sit up now?" Mr. Langford tenderly helped the beauty to do just that. Lady Emma opened her mouth. Her intention was to protest the fact that Mr. Langford's arms were around her daughter. But with a sudden burst of inspiration, she put its position to better use. "Lord Graymarsh, perhaps you could help dear Evelina home. I really do think the sun is too much for—"

"I will see to Miss Crome." Mr. Langford spoke with a firmness that stopped Lady Emma cold and caused his cousin to look at him curiously. Before the dowager could recover, Gerard had scooped Evelina up into his arms and had gone striding off toward Pether Hall with the beauty clinging pathetically, her head nestled against his shoulder.

"Well, really! I must say!" Lady Emma gasped. She stood for a moment, stunned into uncharacteristic indecision. Then she announced, "Upon my word! This will not do!" to no one in particular as she hurried off after her imperiled daughter.

"I'm going fishing," the Prodigy remarked sullenly, still aggrieved over his sister's unreasonableness where balloon ascensions were concerned. With a black look in her direction, he went striding off toward his abandoned fishing pole.

Lord Graymarsh and Miss Romney stood looking at each other. "She's really very nice," Sarah said.

"Who?"

"Miss Crome, of course. If it weren't for her odious mother flinging the poor girl at your head, mortifying her and disgusting you, I expect you two would deal quite well together. She is without doubt the loveliest female I've ever seen. Don't you agree?"

"Yes," he said, a reply that, though given in acquiescence, did not completely satisfy the questioner. His lordship frowned at her. "Miss Romney, are you matchmaking?"

"No, of course not."

"Good. I find Miss Crome's mother more than sufficient in that area."

"I know. Oh, my heavens, th-that fish!" Sarah choked suddenly, and his lordship grinned. "But," she said, sobering, "that's just my point. I do feel terribly sorry for the girl. She needs to marry well, and with that ogre of a mother making such a cake of her, no one gets to really know her. She is a sweet, shy girl who's basically very kind and would, I expect, make some gentleman a perfect wife."

"And just why are you telling me all this?"

"In the interest of fair play, I suppose. I simply hate to see that old—Lady Emma, that is—ruin Evelina's chances of making a good match."

"You refer to me? How surprising. But then, of course, you're thinking of my fortune."

"Of course. She has to have a good income. But she also needs someone who would treat her kindly."

"Thank you for that much. But are you sure I wouldn't beat her? She looked as though she thought I would."

"Oh, it's not you she's afraid of. It's your balloon. And the fear her mother will force her into it. And Lady Emma would! That woman would stop at nothing to see her daughter marry well!" Sarah pulled herself up short and looked a bit embarrassed by her vehemence. "Well, now, Lord Graymarsh, before you give me the setdown you're longing to and tell me all this is none of my affair, I'll say so myself. I merely wanted you to have some idea of the daughter's true character and not be totally prejudiced by her horrid mother. You could do a lot worse than marry Miss Crome." Her voice trailed off. Sarah was confused by the way his lordship was looking at her.

"Thank you," he said dryly. "I'll add you to the long list of people nudging me toward matrimony. And I promise to look at Miss Crome through new eyes now. But your advocacy may come a little late. Improbable as it seems, I think my cousin may be smitten."

"Mr. Langford? But he's out of the question for Miss Crome."

"Oh, I don't know. I'll admit Gerry is a bit of a rake. But underneath it all his heart's in the right place."

"The location of his heart is to no purpose. Mr. Langford hasn't a feather to fly with, has he?"

"Well, no. Not now at least."

"Then that cooks his goose. For people of your class never marry except for personal advancement of some kind."

Gray stooped, picked up a stone, and skipped it across the water. "Miss Romney," he said, sighing, "as I pointed out before, your view of my class is cynical, to say the least."

"But the point I made is accurate?"

"In as far as generalizations can ever be, I suppose so. At least I will not argue the point with you." Indeed, he could not. For the memory of Lord Petherbridge's scheme for the disposal of his fortune had come rushing back to him.

Miss Romney found herself regretting her want of tact. The shuttered look on his lordship's face signaled the end of a conversation she'd enjoyed. Well, it was not surprising that he found her constant attacks upon his upper-class values distasteful. What was harder to account for was the distinct impression on her part that Lord Graymarsh was feeling guilty. She dismissed the notion as absurd.

Chapter Twelve

That evening when the gentlemen joined the ladies in the drawing room, the Petherbridge house party, never rated high by any of the guests, seemed to sink to its lowest point. Perhaps because the solicitous inquiries into Miss Crome's heath had set Lady Stanhope off into a detailed account of her own sufferings, the assembly seemed plunged into gloom. It might have been supposed that a natural reaction to the general mood would be to seek diversion. But the drama group did not excuse itself for rehearsal, the whist players did not deal the cards, and the gentlemen did not seize the opportunity to withdraw for billiards. Instead, the entire party was bunched together in one corner of the elegant, spacious room with a grand pianoforte, which no one deigned to play, as their focal point. Expressions ranged from martyred to vacant to resigned as Lady Stanhope droned on and on.

When her ladyship finally paused for breath between her rheumatism and her biliousness, Lord Petherbridge, who had been nodding, awoke to his duties as host. "And how are the riding lessons coming along, m'dear?" he inquired of his most-neglected guest.

The question took Sarah by surprise. She had been watching Lord Graymarsh, who was watching Mr. Langford, who was watching Miss Crome, and did not realize it was she whom Petherbridge addressed. "I beg your pardon, sir?"

"The riding lessons. The coachman tells me that Gray here has been teaching you and your little brother to ride. How are you getting on?"

Lord Petherbridge had snatched the gathering from its stupor. Randolph and Gerard glowered at Gray. Lady Emma's frown of disapproval was directed at Miss Romney. Lady Stanhope looked peeved at having lost the floor. Lady Petherbridge, Lord Stanhope, Sir Peter, and Miss Crome seemed confused by the currents whirling all around them.

"Giving lessons, are you, Gray?" His lordship's younger brother was studiously polite. Only his eyes accused. "Never knew that sort of thing was your line of country."

"Yes, Gray." Mr. Langford's smile was devoid of warmth. "Do enlighten us. When did this come about?"

Petherbridge answered for him. "Oh, Webster says they've been going out every morning since they got here. How are your pupils doing, Gray?"

"Yes, don't keep us in suspense, Gray. We're on the very edges of our seats. How are you as a riding master?"

"As to that, I couldn't say. Miss Romney and her brother have made excellent progress, but the success lies in their aptitude, not in my teaching."

"I'm sure you are far too modest," his cousin contradicted. "Your dedication must have inspired your pupils. Just think of it, Randolph. Your brother, who professes to have no interest at all in"—he paused for a moment and then continued—"*others*, rises early every morning to ride forth with Miss Romney."

"We were not alone," Sarah protested after Lady Emma had sniffed a telling sniff. "Tidswell has also been a pupil."

"Ah, yes. The Prodigy. You are all heart, Gray," Langford drawled while his lordship glared daggers back at him. "It occurs to me that if you had not been born to your present position, you could have been quite successful as a tutor. There's no end to your talents, is there, Coz? Fishing instructor. Riding master. What will it be next? Sketching? Languages?"

"Dancing!" Lady Emma declared with such resonance that all heads turned her way. "Lord Graymarsh must put his instructive talents to work right here and now." The smile directed toward Graymarsh, while meant to dazzle, was dimmed by yellowed teeth. "I am assured, your lordship, that you are quite accomplished in the new dance craze. I refer to the waltz, of course."

"Indeed? And who would have told you that?"

"Why, it's common knowledge. And I myself have observed that your lordship is particularly skilled in all other modes of dancing, though of course we did not deem the waltz proper at Evelina's come-out. But since Czar Alexander has waltzed at Almack's, it is no longer thought a shocking fad. And one must always keep abreast of fashion. Therefore I am determined that Evelina should learn the waltz. And with a skilled instructor, as I've no doubt your lordship will prove to be, I'm certain my little girl will master it in no time. So, with Lady Augusta's kind permission, I am prepared to play while you lead Evelina through the steps."

"I don't think—" Gray had begun when his brother interrupted. "What a capital idea! Let's all join in. Do you waltz, Miss Romney?"

"Well, yes, but—"

"I am sure Miss Romney wishes to pursue her dramatic duties." Lady Emma dared anyone to differ.

"Ah, yes, but you really should take advantage of Randolph's enthusiasm." Gerard was unperturbed by a frosty look. "Actually he is a much more accomplished dancer than his older brother. I hope you take no offense, Gray."

"I try not to, Cousin."

"Oh, but I am sure that Miss Romney requires Mr. Milbanke's presence at the rehearsal, whereas Evelina's and Lord Graymarsh's parts are so insignificant that their presence would scarce be missed. Is that not so, Miss Romney?"

"Well, actually, if no one really wishes to rehearse, I suppose we might forgo it this one evening," Sarah said doubtfully.

"Not wish it?" With an effort, Gerard forced his thoughts away from the lovely Miss Crome and the memory of her arms clasped around his neck. He thought instead of her nonexistent fortune and of his uncle's wealth. Thus fortified, he contrived to seize the moment and turn it to his advantage. "I personally cannot face losing even one evening's practice without being beset by an onslaught of the quakes." His drawling tone gave no evidence of his inward state. "As you well know, Miss Romney, the success or failure of *The Gamester* is largely in our hands. That fact may not cause you trepidation—you are, after all, a professional—but I can assure you that the prospect fills me with terror. And Lady Emma is right, as usual. Miss Crome and Gray do not need as much rehearsal as we do. Nor does Randolph. So why don't we leave the brothers here to teach Miss Crome the waltz while we go to the theater and run through our scenes."

Sarah did not like the suggestion. Nor did Randolph and Gray look very pleased. Evelina was obviously upset. "Perhaps we should all go practice." The beauty showed rare spunk.

"Nonsense." Her mother overrode her easily. "As Mr. Langford has pointed out, minor characters do not need as much rehearsal as leading ones."

Sarah was still trying to find an acceptable alternative to Gerard's proposal when Lord Petherbridge spoke up dismissively. "That's settled, then. Gerard, you and Miss Romney go rehearse."

Reminded of her status, Sarah felt her face go red. She rose slowly to her feet, reluctant to be alone with Mr. Langford and made even more uneasy by the suspicious look in Graymarsh's eyes as he studied his handsome cousin. But Lord Petherbridge had made her position abundantly clear. She was not a guest. She was a hired performer.

In truth, such a setdown had been the furthest thing from Lord Petherbridge's mind. He'd been uncharacteristically quick to realize that Gerard was maneuvering a chance to be alone with Sarah. And though Mr. Langford was not his lordship's first choice as a secret son-in-law, he had to admire the skill with which Gerard disposed of his two rivals. Lord Petherbridge's single-minded concern was that a nephew win Miss Romney. And so far as he could tell, not one of the slow-tops was making any progress. He did wish that somebody would get on with the job and bring an end to this infernal house party and leave him in peace. Hence his willingness to aid and abet Gerard. He rose to his feet to organize a table of cards, "as far away from that blasted waltz music as possible."

Sarah was on the point of excusing herself to go get Tidswell to hold the prompt book when she remembered that Tids was spending the evening conning a selection from *Practical Piety.* Lady Petherbridge had decreed that the Prodigy recite Miss More's work at the end of their performance as a sort of antidote to *The Gamester* and a salve to her conscience for allowing such questionable entertainment to take place. Poor Tidswell had been too frightened of her ladyship to offer any objection. In spite of Sarah's promise, it seemed that he was to perform after all.

"I hope you don't mind giving me this extra time." As they entered the theater, Mr. Langford appeared to read Sarah's thoughts. His blue eyes held a glint of amusement at her obvious discomfort at being alone with him. He looked even more handsome than usual in his black evening coat and white knee smalls.

"No, of course not. Indeed, I am quite impressed with your dedication."

He didn't miss the irony. "Oh, I really am quite dedicated. But whether the dedication is to the play or to the leading lady is a question I have not allowed myself to explore."

Sarah took refuge in professionalism and bustled about the stage arranging rehearsal props. "Is there some particular spot you're having problems with, Mr. Langford?" she asked in a firm, directorial voice, then could have cut her tongue out.

But much to her relief, he did not choose the love scene. True, the part he claimed to find difficult did lead up to their embrace. Sarah planned to bring the rehearsal to a halt at least a page and a half before that intimacy.

She did not plan for her artistic nature to get the upper hand of her good sense. But she soon immersed herself in the role of Mrs. Beverley, forgetting all else in the pleasure of playing opposite an actor of Mr. Langford's skill. Sarah dimly recognized that she had never performed better and began to wonder if, unhampered by the third-rate Romney players, she might not aspire to the stature of a Mrs. Siddons. It was in this euphoric state that she allowed herself to be swept on past the stopping place and ended up involved once more in an out-of-control love scene.

"Beverley! How dare you!" It said something for Sarah's state of mind that when she finally struggled free from an embrace that left her red of face and angry, she was still in character. The look of amusement on Mr. Langford's face brought her back to reality. She made an effort to retrieve the director's authority he'd usurped along with her dignity. "I think we've rehearsed quite long enough."

"Oh, but I disagree." They had moved, appropriately, front and center. He reached for her again. She sidestepped quickly. Sarah's next impulse was to leap over the footlights and go sprinting for the door. Instead, she elected to face him down. The ambivalence seemed to amuse him even more. "No need to look so Friday-faced, Sarah love. Why not admit it? You enjoyed our rehearsal as much as I did."

"Oh, I admit it. Up to a point."

"And just what point was that?"

"When you dropped out of character and developed an extra set of hands, that's when. Mr. Langford, you are well aware that the scene, as you've just played it, wouldn't be allowed in Covent Garden, let alone in Lady Petherbridge's private theatricals."

"Oh, I intend to tone my performance down. Don't distress yourself on that score, love. But while we're alone, I see no reason to hide my true feelings." He moved toward her and she backed away. "Come now, Sarah." His voice was seductive. "Don't be such a tease. You must know how I feel by now."

"I most certainly do know," she retorted. "I not only know how you feel: I know where you feel, and I'm warning you that if you ever try those tricks again when we're rehearsing, I'll—I'll—" She sputtered to an impotent stop, unable to think of a threat with any substance to it.

He laughed huskily and pulled her into his arms again. At first she struggled, then, being no match for him in strength, sighed faintly and succumbed, melting against him, holding her slightly parted lips tilted upward to be kissed. There was a sparkle of triumph in his eyes as he bent his head to meet them. His lips teased, then grew insistent. Just before she wound up being caught in her own trap, Miss Romney stamped with all her might upon her lover's arch.

"Ow! Dammit! Ow!" Mr. Langford howled and pirouetted, clasping both hands around his injured foot while his thumbs explored the throbbing spot beneath his silken hose. "You vixen! You've broken it!"

"With these soft slippers? I think not, more's the pity. But if you're sufficiently cooled off now, Mr. Langford, I do believe you owe me an explanation for your conduct. Please notice that I did not say apology. For since I am not a lady, I don't suppose that you'd agree I'm due one. But neither am I a lightskirt. Pray in future bear that in mind. Now I await your explanation."

Gerard had sunk down upon one of the chairs that did temporary duty as windows, doors, and furniture upon the stage. He was massaging his damaged foot gingerly. It was hard to tell whether the grimace on his handsome face was for the pain he was suffering or the smudge upon his stocking. Sarah briefly considered making a dignified exit. Instead, she pulled up a chair to face him. "Would you care to explain just what all that groping was in aid of, Mr. Langford?"

"I should think that was obvious, Miss Romney," he growled.

"Not to me it wasn't." She paused then and looked thoughtful. "I suppose the logical explanation is that when a man finds himself in an intimate situation with a woman—any woman—it's his second nature to take liberties. Take your cousin's reaction in the Plymouth inn, for instance. It was exactly the same sort of thing. And I expect this kind of conduct is especially true of gentlemen of your class."

Gerard gave her a cool stare. No love light could be seen glowing in his eyes. "I feel I'm going to hate myself for asking, but why my class in particular?"

"Well, for one thing, you are accustomed to taking whatever you want as your unquestioned right. For another, I expect your type is rather unsure of your own manhood."

Mr. Langford's blue eyes narrowed. "What a novel notion. Not many of my acquaintance would dare subscribe to it."

"No need to take offense. I am speaking in general terms. It merely struck me that men of your class are for the most part useless, which undoubtedly is why they're obsessed with boxing in Cribb's Parlour, riding neck-or-nothing, hunting, wenching—all the rest. How else would they prove their manhood?"

"Since the activities you describe aren't limited to the ton, except perhaps in scope of opportunity, I find your thesis a little lacking, Miss Romney. Not to say bird-witted."

"Well, perhaps you're right, Mr. Langford. If so, we are back where this conversation started. I've no earthly notion then why you chose to behave as you just did."

Perhaps only a stage-trained observer would have noticed him ease back into character, so subtle was the transformation. Even Sarah came close to being dazzled by his slow, seductive smile. She had to remind herself that mere seconds before Mr. Langford had longed to throttle her. "Sarah, Sarah," he said, still using her first name with no by-you-leave, "why are you so determined to come up with all these daft explanations for my actions and ignore the obvious? Surely it's crossed your mind that I'm falling in love with you."

"Fustian!"

The flat retort took some of the wind out of his sails, but he quickly rallied. "Oh, come now, Sarah. You are not as indifferent toward me as you'd like to pretend. Can you deny you felt some response to my lovemaking—cold, heartless Sarah?"

"Of course I don't deny it." Her face grew warm at the recollection. "But I know as well as you do that it had nothing to do with love."

"Perhaps not on your part," he answered huskily. "But you have no right to weigh my feelings on the scale of your own indifference. Why can you not simply believe that I love you?"

"Well . . ." She took his question seriously and turned it over in her mind. "I could give you any number of good reasons, but I'll boil them down to two. First, I am an actress. And I recognize a performance when I see it. Oh, a good performance, I give you that much credit. I think you could have a glorious stage career, Mr. Langford, if you chose to. But your lovemaking was a performance all the same.

"And my second reason may also have to do with my stage training. At least I like to pride myself that I'm more observant than most. You see, I've seen the way you look at Miss Crome when you think you're unobserved. I think you're in love with her."

"And I think you, Miss Romney, have the most freakish notions of any person I've ever met. Even your preposterous attack on my manhood is not as absurd as that. My being in love with Miss Crome is not merely ridiculous: it's unthinkable."

"Well, as to that," Sarah answered slowly, "I'm sure you're right. Speaking practically, that is. But when did 'ridiculous' and 'unthinkable' ever have anything to say in the matter of falling in love? Now, marriage is another thing entirely."

"That's a very astute observation." From the back of the theater, a voice interrupted—brittle, sophisticated, and amused. "I await your comments with bated breath, Gerry darling."

The onstage characters were startled into getting to their

feet. Neither had heard the newcomer's entrance and had no idea how long she'd stood there listening.

Lady Scriven, as conscious as any actress of the effect that she was having, walked slowly down the aisle. She was not a beauty of the first rank. She was certainly beyond the blush of youth. Few would ever notice either fact.

She was elegantly dressed in black crape over a sarsnet slip. Her hair, black as her adornments, was lightly covered by a long veil draped over a jeweled aigrette. In contrast to all the dramatic inkiness, her milk-white complexion appeared luminous, her lavender eyes intense. All in all, Sarah thought, she'd never seen a more striking woman. She disliked her immediately.

The interloper seated herself front-row center and looked up at the stage expectantly. "Pray do not let me interrupt your little scene. You were *rehearsing*, were you not?" The lips curved mockingly.

"Lucy, what the devil are you doing here?" Mr. Langford was jolted from his usual savoir faire.

The lady's eyebrows rose. Her amusement increased. "Why, Gerard, what an uncivil question. One could almost suppose, my dear, that you are not pleased to see me. But to give an answer that your rudeness does not deserve, I'm here because Lady Petherbridge invited me. Did I fail to mention that fact in London?" she asked innocently.

"As a matter of fact, you did say you were asked." In an effort to regain composure, Mr. Langford helped himself to snuff. "But I thought you had not planned to come."

"Did you, indeed? What a strange coincidence. I had the same impression about you." The voice purred, but the lavender eyes narrowed just a bit. "You were not by chance, Gerry darling, trying to put me off?"

"Of course I was." He had full command of himself once more. "Tried to do you a favor. Knew you'd find the place tedious beyond redemption. I hadn't intended to come myself. Sent my regrets, in fact. But the old gentleman wouldn't hear of my crying off. And I can hardly afford to cross him, so . . ." He shrugged elegantly.

Her smile was as false as his explanation. "You are the most accomplished liar I know, Gerry dear. Perhaps that's why I find you so amusing. But pray get on with . . . whatever you were doing." Her gaze shifted to Miss Romney. It made Lady Emma's similar appraisal seem almost approving.

Sarah turned to Mr. Langford. "I think that will be sufficient rehearsal for the evening, Gerry," she said coolly, using his first name just to be annoying. "Now, if you will excuse me." Without waiting for an introduction to the newcomer, she swept off the stage and up the auditorium aisle. She thought she did it very well, but her "Mrs. Siddons, famous actress" bubble was burst by the look of contemptuous amusement she glimpsed on the widow's face as she breezed on by her. All in all, Lady Scriven was the last straw in a thoroughly trying day.

Her solace was, Sarah concluded, as she decided to forgo the society in the withdrawing room and headed for her bedchamber instead, that those two sophisticates back in the theater deserved each other. But then she thought of Miss Crome with a sigh. She was almost certain that the beauty was falling in love with Mr. Langford. Why did females insist upon forming *tendres* for the most unsuitable members of the other sex? And with that poser, the vision of Lord Graymarsh took over center stage in her imaginings. "Oh, fiddle!" Miss Romney said explosively as she slammed her chamber door. "A pox on all of them!"

Chapter Thirteen

Sarah was not surprised when Lord Graymarsh failed to put in an appearance the next morning at the stables. Although she'd been puzzled by the reactions when the rest of the party discovered he'd been teaching Tids and her to ride, she did realize that the disclosure was going to put a period to the lessons. What she had not expected was that Randolph would take his brother's place.

The grooms were leading their horses up and down while Randolph stood by a marble watering trough, flicking his boot with his riding whip. It had taken a bit of courage to face Sarah. Since the embarrassing bedchamber scene, he'd done his best to avoid her. But now he was determined to put himself back into contention for his uncle's fortune. The time was ripe. Gray, whose clandestine meetings with the heiress were most suspicious, had seemed grateful nonetheless when he'd offered to substitute as riding master. And Lady Scriven's unexpected arrival had effectively disposed of Gerry. Randolph had a clear field and intended to make the most of it. He forced a smile as the Romneys approached. "Here you are, finally. You had me worried. I was afraid you weren't going to ride this morning."

"Oh, Sarah dropped her stupid glove along the path and didn't notice for ever so long and we had to go back and hunt for it." Tidswell sounded quite disgusted. "I told her we could just as well look when we came back. Ain't as if it's likely to rain or anything." Indeed, the weather remained amazingly fine. The morning air was cool and pleasant. "Can't see why she couldn't just as well ride with one glove as two. Oh, I say, where's Lord Graymarsh?"

"He won't be coming this morning. I'm taking over his pleasant duty."

Tidswell's look of disappointment was hardly flattering. Nor was the "Oh, blast!" the boy muttered under his breath.

"Tidswell!" his shocked sister exclaimed. "Do beg Mr. Milbanke's pardon."

"Oh, it ain't that I mind him being here," Tidswell said sulkily. "It's just that I particularly wished to ask Gray something."

Sarah, even more embarrassed, was about to lecture her brother upon the shocking familiarity of calling Lord Graymarsh by his shortened name when Randolph forestalled her by saying, "Well, if your question has anything to do with that infernal balloon, Tids, I think Gray means to work on it this morning."

"He does? This morning? Oh, I say, how marvelous! Do you suppose he'd let me go with him, sir? I'm sure I could be useful." Tidswell's eyes were filled with longing.

"Well, of course it ain't up to me to say, but I should think Gray would welcome your company. For it ain't often that he finds anyone to share his enthusiasm. His family's more inclined to pour cold water on his scheme."

That was all the permission the Prodigy needed. Pausing only to pop a sugar lump into his horse's mouth and to give the animal a pat on the nose and a promise to see it tomorrow, the boy was off, responding to his sister's shouted "Tidswell! I really don't think you should!" by running all the harder.

Sarah turned to Randolph in despair. "Oh, dear. I'm afraid his lordship won't be pleased."

"Nonsense. I meant what I said. Gray'll be glad of his company." His forced smile turned suddenly mischievous. "He'll be almost as pleased to have him there as I am."

"Am I to understand that you were trying to get rid of poor Tidswell?"

They were moving out of the stableyard. Randolph, who took his duties seriously, observed her closely. Only when assured of her competence as a horsewoman did he resume their conversation. "You mustn't say 'poor Tidswell.' It's nothing against the boy if I wish to be alone with his lovely, charming, talented sister."

Randolph, Sarah noted, was quite pleased with that fulsome speech. She chose to overlook it. But after several more callow attempts at gallantry, his flowery periods began to pall. For some unfathomable reason, Randolph seemed determined, once again, to turn himself into a poor imitation of his Don Juan cousin. It only needed the gold dressing gown! Sarah did wish he'd revert to his own personality, which really was quite likable. She was just about to say so when she recalled his youth. Coming on the heels of his midnight misadventure, such a comment might prove crushing. As an alternative to plain speaking, she urged her horse into a brisk canter that broke up their tête-à-tête.

Sarah slowed her horse to a walk as they climbed a grassy mound. Randolph reined in beside her. When he addressed her this time, she was relieved to note, it was as himself. "I say, Sarah—oh, may I call you that?"

"Of course."

"Good. You call me Randolph. It will make things easier."

What things? she wondered, and was about to ask when he forestalled her.

"I say, Sarah, could we get off and talk a bit? Seriously, I mean."

She was totally mystified now and a bit alarmed by his expression. His young face had grown quite intense; one could say it almost looked harried. Although the morning was still on the cool side, tiny beads of perspiration glistened on his forehead. What on earth can be wrong? she wondered as she dismounted. Oh, my goodness, I'll bet a monkey he has stage fright and is trying to find the courage to tell me he won't do the play.

So when Randolph took her by the hand, led her over to a fallen log underneath a spreading oak, and bade her to sit down a moment while he spoke to her, her mind was busily sorting out proper phrases of reassurance. "Everyone gets butterflies at the thought of performance. It's only natural and soon passes." Or "But Randolph, you have made such splendid progress in your role. You must not—" Her thoughts were interrupted. Mr. Milbanke had suddenly gone down on one knee in front of her and was clasping his hands in supplication.

"What on earth!" she exclaimed. Then she thought, Well, really, there was no need to make a Cheltenham tragedy of the thing. If he felt that strongly about dropping the part . . .

"Miss Romney—Sarah." The sweat on Randolph's brow was increasing. "I know my declaration may come as a shock to you. But I can no longer hold my tongue."

"Well, after all, Randolph, if you feel you positively cannot appear, then I suppose—"

Randolph rolled over the interruption lest it divert him from the set speech he'd been practicing in his head throughout a long and sleepless night. "Forgive my abruptness in declaring myself. But I fear I may not soon find another opportunity to be alone with you. And the depth of my passion demands utterance, dear, dear Sarah."

"The depth of your what?" Her look of astonishment rather threw him off his stride.

"My passion," he said awkwardly.

"For me?" Her tone was rife with disbelief.

"Of course, you." Randolph was nettled by all these interruptions. They interfered with his train of thought. "Do you see anyone else around?"

"Randolph, is this some sort of joke?"

"No, dammit. I'm making you an offer. That is, I would be if you'd let me get on with it. I had the thing all worked out and now it's gone clear out of my head."

"An offer! Randolph, how old are you?" Sarah might have looked the same way at Tidswell caught in some transgression.

"How old am I?" Exasperation was getting the upper hand. "Nineteen. But what has that to say to anything?"

"Isn't nineteen a trifle young to be thinking of offering a carte blanche? Not to say that such a thing would be proper at any age."

"A carte blanche! Who mentioned a carte blanche? Such a thought never entered my head. My God, how could you be thinking I'd be offering a carte blanche? Why, I could never afford—that is, what I mean to say is, I would never . . . Dammit, Sarah, you've caused me to make a complete mull of my marriage proposal."

"Marriage? You're asking me to marry you? *Marry* you? I don't believe it!"

"I know it's sudden and all. But I may never get a better chance to be alone with you." He reached for her hand

and gave it a tender squeeze. "Sarah, do say you'll be mine."

"Randolph, do please get up off your knees and stop talking nonsense." She tried to take some of the sting out of her words by smiling, though in truth she longed to box the young man's ears. "I don't know what sort of maggot you've got in your head, but I do wish you'd get rid of it and let us get on with our ride."

"Sarah." The pressure of his handclasp was intended to be ardent. She would have called it painful. "I love you, Sarah."

Miss Romney sighed. Really, this sort of thing was getting to be outside of enough. "You do no such thing."

She sounded much like a governess even to her own ears, and more so to Randolph's. It was appallingly clear to the young man that things were not going at all as planned. Well, then. If words would not convince her, he'd just have to take a page from his cousin Gerard's book and arouse her carnal passions. No sooner had the thought occurred than he was beside her on the log, crushing her in his arms and kissing her clumsily. Unfortunately, the very suddenness of his assault, coupled with her desire to elude the embrace, sent Miss Romney reeling backward. Equally off balance, striving—unsuccessfully—not to terminate the kiss, Randolph tumbled on top of her. His cousin Gerard would not have been deterred by such a circumstance. That beau would have simply reembraced and started over. But Randolph found the fact that Miss Romney was suffering a giggling fit entirely offputting. The devil with Gerry, anyhow!

"I don't think that's a very proper way to act when a cove has just offered you his heart," he said sullenly, wiping the dirt off his buckskins and riding coat.

"I'm so s-sorry," she gurgled. "But you must admit, we did look ridiculous."

"Thank you very much."

"Oh, come now, Randolph," she chided, settling her cork hat straight and shaking out her skirt to rid it of debris. "Please don't put yourself into a taking. Things could be a lot worse, you know. Why, I might even have taken your proposal seriously."

"Dammit, I was serious!"

"Were you?" She looked at him speculatively. "If so, I wonder why." He reddened a bit, and she continued. "For you've not the slightest wish to be married to me. I'd stake my life on it."

"That's not true. I do wish it. The thing is, I happen to like you a lot."

"And I like you, too. But that's no reason to get married. So may I suggest that we simply drop the subject and continue with our ride?"

Randolph opened his mouth to protest, mumbled, "Oh, blast!" instead, and shut it again. It was obvious he'd made a shambles of the thing. Still, he thought with youthful optimism as they remounted and set off at a sedate pace, at least the ice was broken. She now knew he wished to marry and not seduce her. That should erase the bad impression he'd made by sneaking into her chamber and scaring her half to death. And once she got over the shock of his unexpected proposal and thought it over, she was bound to reconsider. After all, as far as she knew, he was a damn fine catch for her. Or any actress. Well above her touch in the ordinary way of things. But he would have to fix the matter right and tight before Gerry made his move. Better not put it off too long. Couldn't depend on Lady Scriven keeping his cousin occupied forever. Nor could he entirely trust Gray to keep his oar out of the matrimonial waters. By George, he'd propose again tomorrow. Bound to have the hang of it the second time around. Randolph began to whistle under his breath.

Sarah, who'd been stealing worried glances at him as they rode along, was glad to see his spirits so restored. Her conscience was troubling her for laughing at him. Well, laughing at herself, actually. "I don't think I've ever seen a lovelier countryside," she offered as a conversational gambit to ease his mind from the embarrassing incident. "This must be the most beautiful estate in Hampshire."

"I think so." He spoke with great conviction as he surveyed the lush, sloping green hills. "Can you imagine what it would be like to own it?" he asked slyly.

"Indeed I cannot." She laughed. "As an actress, I do live in a world of make-believe, but my imagination doesn't stretch that far. But how about you? It's certainly less far-fetched to ask what you would do if you owned such an estate."

"I'd modernize it," he answered promptly. "Bring in the latest methods of agriculture. Change the fusty notions Uncle clings to. My God, I could double the yield in no time." The young face was alight with enthusiasm.

"Why, Randolph, I'd no idea you were such a farmer."

"I'm not. Got nothing to farm, you see, the way things stand. The land all belongs to Gray."

"And does he share your enthusiasm?"

"Well, yes and no. That is to say, he keeps up with the times. His bailiff's top-rate and gets the best out of the land. So Gray leaves all that sort of thing up to him. He looks after the tenants himself, though: I'll give him that. There's nobody better. But Gray's interests are scientific. Like ballooning. He could drive you insane with all his talk of air currents and temperatures at certain altitudes and hot air as opposed to hydrogen. Before that, he was daft over steam engines."

"Well, could you not run his farm for him?"

"You mean take his bailiff's place? Of course not." From his tone she might as well have suggested he become a highwayman.

Sarah thought it time to change the subject. "Have you

noticed that your cousin seems to be falling in love?'' she asked.

''Gerry?'' He tried to sound nonchalant, but the query jolted him. ''Oh, Gerry's always falling in and out of love. Does it as often as he changes cravat styles. You mustn't take him too seriously. Fickle. That's Cousin Gerard.''

''Really? Well, you certainly know him better than I. But I would have said he's formed a sincere *tendre* for Miss Crome.''

''Miss Crome!'' He reined his horse to a standstill, amazed and relieved at the same time. ''Gerry and Miss Crome? But that's absurd.''

''I don't see why.'' She turned back to let her mount graze a moment beside his. ''Goodness, can you imagine the difficulty those two must have in finding others as dazzling as they? You must admit that as a couple they take the breath away.''

''Yes, but Gerry's pockets are to let and Miss Crome hasn't a feather to fly with. It ain't like him to . . . Well,'' he mused aloud, ''if he is dangling after her, it's just because she's meant for Gray.''

''I don't think I understand.''

''Simple enough. Gerry's green with jealousy over Gray. Always has been. They're the same age, you see. Been thrown together since they were in leading strings. Been rivals ever since Gerry began to understand how much Gray had and how poor his own prospects were. He tries to best Gray in every possible way. So I guess that could include Miss Crome.''

''But that's terrible.''

''Well, it's stupid, anyhow. For what Gerry don't realize is that Gray couldn't care less. At least I don't think he's interested in the fair Evelina,'' he amended. ''But it could cook Gerry's goose if what you say is true and he gets carried away by the thing. Of course, Lady Scriven ain't likely to let that happen. She's got her claws hooked into

Gray. Good thing, too. Gerry has to marry an heiress. He's got no choice.''

Sarah sighed and patted her impatient horse's neck. ''The quality are certainly mercenary. I'll wager that Miss Crome and Mr. Langford could rub along quite well by most people's standards. They might not afford to keep a stable or—''

''Well, you'd lose,'' he interrupted. ''They couldn't rub along well by any standard. Not in debtors' prison. Economies won't help. Gerry's too far up the river Tick for that. If word got out that he'd married just for love, his creditors would flock like vultures. Gerry's a gambler, you see. Bets on anything and everything. Which raindrop will beat the others down the glass. Whether a certain cove will wear a buttonhole that day. Who'll manage to seduce a certain female first— Oh, I do beg pardon.''

''Not at all.'' Sarah's eyes were wide. ''You mean gentlemen would actually place bets upon a thing like that?''

He looked embarrassed. ''Well, yes. Happens all the time, in fact. But I should not have said so. Didn't intend to shock you.''

''Oh, you haven't shocked me. In point of fact, I think you've just enlightened me. I'm very glad to have this insight. I think it may explain— Well, never mind.'' The suspicion that was forming her mind could be explored alone and at her leisure.

As they resumed their ride, Randolph's troubled conscience began nagging him a bit. ''Don't want to give you the wrong idea about Gerry,'' he said abruptly. ''Shouldn't make him out a scoundrel, for he ain't. Oh, what I said is the truth—about him being a gambler and jealous of Gray. He's all of that. But he's got another side. Like my brother says, Gerry might knife you in the back himself, but he'd stop any other cove from doing it.''

''How chivalrous,'' Miss Romney murmured.

Randolph missed the sarcastic overtones. He was too busy mulling over what she'd said. "By George, I guess it is at that. Gerry would have made a real go of that sort of thing. Clanking around in armor. Jousting in tournaments." He went on pursuing that train of thought while Sarah's mind was on another tangent.

The manor house was back in view before she broke their silence. "Randolph, forgive my impertinence, but I've been thinking. Do you have any money of your own at all?"

Randolph's eyes sparkled at the question. By Jove, she was having second thoughts about his proposal! "A little," he answered. "And, of course, I do have some prospects."

"But I'm not talking about when this or that person should die. I mean, do you have enough brass, er, money, that is to say, to purchase a small farm right now?"

"Well, yes, I collect so."

"Then why don't you simply buy one and farm it yourself? Why, with your expert knowledge, I should think you'd make a success of it in no time."

His jaw dropped. She might have made an indecent proposal of some kind. "You mean you want me to be a *farmer*?"

"It's not what *I* want. It's you I'm thinking of. Doing something positive with your life. Isn't that what you'd like to do? Farm, I mean?"

"You must be bamming me." He looked shocked. "It simply ain't done, you know."

"No." She sighed. "I suppose it isn't. But somehow it does seem a pity."

They finished the ride in silence, both deep in depressing thoughts.

Chapter Fourteen

Sarah was more than willing the next morning to join in the excursion to watch Graymarsh attempt to put his balloon back in the air. She needed the distraction. Yesterday's conversation with Randolph had cleared up a mystery but left her decidedly blue-deviled.

There was no further doubt in her mind that she was the object of a wager. Mr. Langford and Randolph were in competition to see who could seduce her first. What, she wondered, was the stake? No, on second thought, she'd rather not know her value. Was it recorded in White's notorious betting book?

Anger might follow, but at the moment she was simply disillusioned. She was especially disappointed in Randolph Milbanke. That he should engage in such a business at all was unthinkable. But to dangle marriage like a carrot . . .

that was reprehensible! Well, the ways of the ton were incomprehensible. Not to mention downright immoral. The sooner she could leave Pether Hall the better. She wished she'd never come. She almost wished that three young gentlemen of the ton had never entered the stage box of the Portsmouth Theatre.

Sarah was not the only one to welcome a diversion. The entire Petherbridge house party seemed to be sunk in despondency. Lady Scriven's arrival could have contributed to Miss Crome's dejection. And if, underneath his usual nonchalance, Mr. Langford was indeed furious, again Lady Scriven must bear the blame. But why Lady Emma should be out of sorts, Lady Stanhope suffering all her complaints at once, Lord Stanhope fidgety, and Sir Peter cross, was past understanding. Even the ebullient Randolph Milbanke appeared sunk in the general gloom. So when the Prodigy had come rushing in at breakfast to announce, "Have you heard? Gray—I mean to say, his lordship—plans to try his balloon today!" the whole party had come to life.

The day was bright and sunny with a gentle breeze, propitious for ballooning. The ascension site was within easy walking distance of the manor house. Servants were immediately dispatched with the provisions deemed necessary for the party's comfort and refreshment, and the guests set forth on foot soon after breakfast.

Sarah looked around in vain for the Prodigy. She had started back to find him when Randolph stopped her. "Don't be silly. He won't be there. You surely can't think Gray's been able to take a step all day without the boy right on his heels. Come on. It would be just like my brother to start without us and spoil the only bit of excitement we've any hope of."

The two of them fell into step with Miss Crome and her mother. Sarah was well aware that Lady Emma did not want her daughter associating with an actress, but the poor girl looked unhappy and in need of a friend. There was little doubt that the sight of Lady Scriven and Mr. Langford walking on ahead, with the lady's hand placed possessively on the gentleman's arm, was the main source of the beauty's misery. That and her mother's satisfaction at the sight.

"Mr. Milbanke, you must be very proud of your adventurous brother." Lady Emma beamed at Randolph. At the same time, she managed not to see Sarah at all. "Evelina and I were just remarking about how greatly we admire these intrepid aeronauts."

"Do you, ma'am?" Randolph's eyebrows ascended in surprise. "I've always held the opinion they're bedlamites myself."

"It does seem terribly dangerous." Miss Crome shivered. "Is Tidswell going up, Miss Romney?"

"Oh, no. And he'll never forgive me for not allowing it. He went over my head and wrote to our father. But, thank goodness, Papa was even more horrified at the notion than I was and flatly refused to give permission."

Randolph barely kept his face straight. "I'll bet a monkey he told Tids that a talent like his must be guarded for posterity or some such thing."

"You are exactly on target." Sarah chuckled, and Randolph felt free to release his grin.

When they arrived, the meadow looked like a scientific laboratory gone slightly mad. Even the cows appeared fascinated by what was going on. While they had prudently retreated to a safe distance, they'd ceased to graze and stood staring at the center of activity, chewing their cuds with that bovine passivity that is as close as cows can come to curiosity.

A huge mass of crumpled silk lay in the center of the field. Gray, Tids, and three burly gardeners were busily unloading casks of hydrogen and yards of hose pipe from a cart and placing them near the silver silk. This accomplished, a rubber umbilical cord was stretched between the cask and the collapsed balloon. The inflation process began.

Sarah shared none of Lady Emma's admiration for the "intrepid" aeronauts. She was, in fact, terrified for Lord Graymarsh's safety. It was her secret hope that there would be some defect in the balloon, left over from its unauthorized descent into the lake. A small tear, perhaps, that had gone undetected but that would suffice to prevent inflation. It had been a frail hope, and it soon expired. The mass of silk writhed sensuously on the ground, puffed a bit like yeasty dough, and then began to fill in earnest.

"Ooooh!" Even the timid Evelina Crome was moved to gasp in admiration as the balloon slowly took shape and began to rise above its boat, like an outsized bird venturing out of the nest to try the air. Up and up it rose, its crimson-bordered, bright blue band unfolding in all its bravery as the silken orb filled out, became tightly packed, and tugged against the ropes that kept it earthbound.

"Huzzah!" Tids shouted as he danced up and down like some North American tribesman in a ritual celebration.

"Huzzah!" the house-party spectators echoed back, with Sarah cheering and clapping as loudly as anyone, elated at the triumph against all instinct and better judgment.

The house party pressed nearer to inspect the colorful curiosity. Their ranks had been swelled by workers from the fields. Servants streamed toward the meadow from the manor house. Lord and Lady Petherbridge benignly turned blind eyes toward their flagrant truancy.

"Tidswell! You get right out of there!"

The Prodigy had climbed into the blue and crimson boat and was staring upward at the glory. He was the very picture of a fledgling aeronaut with his eye upon the future.

"It's all right." Lord Graymarsh, in consultation with his helpers about recovering the balloon, turned to reassure the Prodigy's sister. "I told him he might get in to get the feel of the thing. Never fear. I'll toss him out before I go."

He smiled away her concern. She found herself smiling back at him.

The sudden warmth and total unexpectedness of her response was almost Gray's undoing. He stifled the impulse to sweep Miss Romney off her feet, toss her into the boat, and go soaring off into the sky with her. Instead, he reluctantly broke off contact with those lovely, extraordinary eyes and turned to continue his instructions.

Sarah, too, had trouble dealing with the moment. She also turned away, back toward the balloon, where her little brother was stooped over, fascinated, it would appear, with the craft's moorings. So absorbed was she in sorting out her confused emotions that it took a while for the significance of her brother's actions to register. "Tids! What are you doing? Stop this instant!" Lunging for the boat, Sarah grasped hold of what in a proper seagoing vessel would have been the bow with some insane idea of preventing its ascent.

"Jump, Sarah, jump!" Tidswell yelled as the balloon began to rise and the crowd around—below—them let out a concerted gasp. "No! Don't jump! Dear heaven, no!" The Prodigy amended in a shriek. "'It's too late now. Hang on, Sarah! Don't panic! I'll haul you in."

The horrified spectators stood frozen in tableau as Miss Romney's boots dangled, kicking, in the air. They watched them inch slowly upward while the balloon, as if to mock the snail's pace of the footwear, rose at an alarming rate. Then with a final kick the boots disappeared over the boat's side. There was just time for the crowd to expel their collective breath before Miss Romney's head was sighted, the merest dot, peering down at them.

"Oh, my God!" Lord Graymarsh croaked as pandemonium broke out. Some of the female servants began to scream. Lady Stanhope suffered palpitations. Miss Crome emitted a soft little moan and crumpled at her mother's feet. Lady Emma bent to succor her only child and was rudely pushed aside by Mr. Langford. He knelt beside the beauty, all anxious concern, and began to chafe her wrists, a technique he was fast perfecting. Lady Scriven, ignoring the runaway balloonists, observed this tender scene with narrowed eyes.

"Dear God, Gray, what can we do?" Randolph shouted as his brother began to race toward the cart that had hauled the casks of hydrogen. "Help me unharness this horse," Gray shouted back as he began uncoupling the animal from the wagon, all the while keeping an eye on the heavens. "I think the little fiend knows what he's about," he muttered as the balloon seemed to taper off its ascent gradually.

"Dear God, I hope so," Randolph breathed prayerfully from the other side.

"He's certainly asked enough questions to be an expert. Lord, what a fool I've been." Gray groaned as he pulled the reluctant dray animal away from its nuncheon of grass and climbed onto its bare back.

"What do you think you're doing?"

"Going after them, of course. Thank God there's no wind. He shouldn't go too far. That is if he can do what I'd planned to do, which was no more than get it up for a test and then right back down again. I'd hoped to bring it down at Pope Farm. There's more level ground there than anywhere else around here. Randolph, you get the landau and head there. Bring bandages, laudanum, smelling salts—whatever. Take Meadow Lane. That should bring you somewhere near my landing site—if the lad can find it and manage to bring the thing down. Oh, God! Don't just stand there—run!"

Randolph sprinted in the direction of Pether Hall as Gray gave the nag a swift kick with his boot heel. It lumbered off while his lordship's eyes fixed themselves on the balloon, an ill-mounted wise man following the natal star.

The aeronauts, after their shaky start, were having the best of it. When first hoisted on board, Sarah's initial shock had been rapidly followed by hysteria. "Oh, my goodness, Tidswell, Papa will kill you! And then he'll kill me for allowing you to get us into this scrape!"

"Now, Sarah, just stay calm. It won't help matters at all for you to go into one of your high flights." Tidswell choked suddenly and giggled. " 'One of your high flights'! Did you hear what I just said?" He whooped.

"I heard," his sister said, groaning at the ill-timed pun, then giggled, too. Tids's absurdity had snatched her back from panic. She was filled with a soothing calm. If these were to be their final moments, well, she'd make the most of them, treasure each fleeting second. She'd take her cue from an intrepid Tids, who was going about the business of ballooning with enthusiastic gusto.

"Would you look at that," she commented as she peered over the side of their swaying craft. "The people are all staring up at us and they're shrinking to nothing as they do so."

"That's because we're going upward, stoopid."

"Funny. It doesn't seem that way at all. It appears as if they are going away from us."

"By George, it does!" Tids paused in his valve inspection to join her view. "Gray said it would be this way," he crowed.

The crowd in the meadow shrank away to tiny ants, then were no more as the balloon drifted and the two Romneys gawked at the awesome prospect far below them. Fields, hedgerows, canals, forests, blended into a mosaic—a winsome pattern put together by some craftsman with an eye for green in all its variations. "Oh, it's beautiful," Sarah breathed just before they were enveloped by a dense, damp fog that totally obliterated the view and caused her to exclaim, "Oh, my goodness, Tids, what's happening?"

"We're in a cloud, that's all." Her brother spoke soothingly. "Nothing to worry about." She was just about to observe that that was as calf-witted a statement as she'd ever heard when suddenly they drifted free and were back in the sunshine once again.

"See, what did I tell you?"

Sarah had only a moment's thankfulness for their deliverance before they shot suddenly upward, tossed by some mischievous airborne giant playing with a ball. Sarah let out a shriek as Tidswell yelled, "We've hit an air current," and jumped to operate the valve that controlled the hydrogen.

Far down below them, fear clutched at Lord Graymarsh as he watched the balloon rapidly gain altitude. "Oh, my God," he said, groaning aloud, "they'll freeze." He kicked his plodding nag viciously, urging it on, as if by sheer force of will he could turn it into Pegasus and go flying after the wayward balloon.

There was a sudden pain in Sarah's ears and she began to shiver. "I sh-should have worn something w-w-warmer than my riding habit had I known," she remarked through chattering teeth, hugging and slapping herself.

"Hang on," said Tids. "I'm going to try to bring her down a bit." As he worked the valve, they plummeted. Sarah felt her stomach drop out from under her and her ears gave a horrendous pop.

"Oh, my God! Oh, please!" Lord Graymarsh, riding with his neck craned upward, combined prayer with expletive.

"Oh, my heavens!" Sarah gasped, then giggled hysterically. "Tids, there goes another pun!"

Her brother's mind was on other things. "It's all right now. I think I've got the hang of it." He began to breathe normally again as they stablized.

Down on terra firma, Graymarsh shouted his relief. "Good lad!" The nag, thinking the annoyance on its back referred to it, stepped up its snail's pace.

The aeronauts floated leisurely for a while enjoying the view until Sarah forced herself to put into words the fear niggling at her. "Tids, do you have the slightest notion of how to get us down?"

"Of course I have." Sarah would have been more reassured if the bravado in his voice had not reminded her of his most successful stage role. "Keep your eye out for a meadow near a crossroads. That's where Gray planned to come down. He said it was the biggest, levelest spot around."

"I'm certainly in favor of that," his sister commented, squinting over the side. "Oh, Tids, there's no cleared place down there that looks any larger than a counterpane. I never realized that England possessed so many trees."

"Those counterpanes are acres wide, dummy. It'll be all right. You'll see."

But seconds after this reassurance, atmospheric conditions conspired to belie his words. A stiff breeze sprang up, gathered force, and propelled them at an alarming rate back in the direction they'd just come from. Tids frantically opened the valve again, and they began to descend out of the current's force. He heaved a sigh of relief as the balloon slowed down a bit.

But the sudden alteration in the flight plan had taken its toll of his confidence. "We'd better get this thing down in the best place we can find," he muttered. "Sarah, keep a lookout, will you?"

She sensed his anxiety and gulped. "All right," she managed to say as they descended even lower.

Gray watched with horror as the balloon was blown back toward him. He urged his reluctant beast to optimum effort and veered off toward a field that, though not as large or nearly as level as the one he'd chosen, was obviously Tids's best hope. "Bring it down, lad, bring it down," he pleaded aloud, then amended his command to a choked "Up, Tids! Up! Up!" when it looked as if the rapidly descending balloon was headed straight for a row of trees.

Sarah's scream warned Tidswell of the danger. He threw

out some of the sand on board for ballast, and the balloon rose a hairs-breadth above the branches as Graymarsh croaked, "Thank God!"

The silver orb descended rapidly once again and came skimming low across the meadow as Gray and his reluctant steed approached from the other side. "Throw out the grappling iron, Tidswell!" he shouted, with little hope that the lad could hear him. But whether on command or by his own volition, the Prodigy did weigh anchor, seconds before he ran out of field.

For a bit, it seemed that the wind would defeat them. The anchor dragged, making a furrow through the meadow, slowing their progress but not stopping it. Then, just before they seemed doomed to hit the trees on the other side, the grappling iron caught on a bush and held.

Gray leaped off the nag and ran with a speed that put the plodding beast to shame. He grabbed the anchor rope and hung on with all his might, while the slowly deflating silk tugged at it. "Quick! Slide down the rope as close together as you can manage!" he shouted upward.

"You first, Tids. I'm right behind you." With a prayer of thanksgiving for their acrobatic training, Sarah came down on top of Tids, who'd struck Graymarsh with a thud. All three landed in a heap as the balloon, lightened of its load, pulled up the bush and went sailing off to clear the treetops and join the clouds again.

Tidswell leaped to his feet to scream, "Oh, no!" and then chased after the airborne orb.

Graymarsh also rose and pulled Sarah into his arms. His face was pale. His voice shook. "I thought I'd lost you." And being unable to express adequately the horror and the bleakness of that prospect, he abandoned the attempt and held her closer, then met her upturned lips with his.

No sooner was that contact made than Sarah soared again. She shot upward into flight, and all the variegated colors that had reflected and refracted from the vapors congregated around the balloon danced once again before her eyes with renewed intensity. She was light-headed—she was spinning—she was flying—it was glorious—beyond belief. Ballooning was indeed an experience she would not have missed for all the world.

Graymarsh, at last, reluctantly removed his lips from hers. He gazed into her luminous eyes and said huskily, "I love you."

I love you. The very familiarity of the phrase was Sarah's downfall. It forced her consciousness open like a valve and allowed euphoria to escape. She'd heard the words too often. She knew their false and hollow ring. Her high flight was finished. She experienced once again the terrible sinking sensation that came from falling too far, too fast. She hit earth with a thud, all her illusions left behind her in the clouds, her feet planted firmly on reality. She gazed up into the nobleman's bemused face as he observed this transformation. "I love you, Sarah," Gray repeated in case she'd failed to comprehend.

"I heard you," she replied as she sadly freed herself from his embrace. " 'Et tu, Brute?' " She sighed.

Chapter Fifteen

"*Oh, sir, it's gone!" Tids wailed, his eyes full of tears.* He'd gone chasing off after the balloon, which had lofted over the woods, with some half-crazed idea that a miracle would send it floating back to where he could snatch the anchor and drag it down. Now, his tail between his legs, he rejoined his sister and Lord Graymarsh. He'd missed all that had passed between them and misinterpreted the bleak look on his lordship's face. "I never meant for this to happen," he said, blubbering. "It's awful. I've gone and l-lost your balloon."

"Good," Gray said tersely. "I never want to see the damned thing again."

"Oh, but you can't really mean that." Sarah had decided that her best course of action was to pretend their kiss had never happened. "I never thought I'd live to hear myself say so—indeed, for a few moments, I never thought I'd live to hear myself say anything—but I can quite see now why you're so enthusiastic about ballooning. It really is quite marvelous. Though not without its hazards." She paled a bit at the memory of the line of trees.

"No, it certainly is not." Lord Graymarsh's usually even-keeled nervous system had suffered too much recent strain. First he'd had to cope with terror. Then with the realization that he was in love. This was rapidly followed by rejection. Now anger was flooding in to add to the devastation of his psyche. "Tidswell, for your sister's sake, I will not give you the hiding you deserve. But when I think that you could have killed Sarah, not to mention broken your own worthless neck . . ." Words failed him, and he shuddered involuntarily.

"Well, you can't blame me for Sarah," the Prodigy said sulkily. "I certainly didn't ask her to come with me."

Graymarsh closed his eyes and the vision of Miss Romney dangling over the side of the rising balloon boat came rushing back. He turned a sickly green. "I take it all back, Tidswell. I may kill you after all. To save me from the gallows, how about you taking that animal back to Pether Hall?" He jerked his head toward the dray horse that was placidly munching grass a few yards away.

Tids looked at it blankly. "How did it get here?"

"I rode it." Gray's voice was grim.

"That bag of bones? It don't look your style at all," the boy said disapprovingly. "Why, it ain't even saddled."

"I noticed that. I may never walk properly again for the chafing that I took, but I managed. And so can you. Ride or lead. I don't care which. Just go before I throttle you."

The Prodigy gave him an uneasy look, decided that he meant it, and, placing his palms on the animal's rump, leaped agilely on its back. The horse looked around to ascertain the source of this new disturbance, then plodded off.

"There's supposed to be a rescue party headed our way," Gray said to Sarah. "We can wait for it or start walking, just as you please."

"Oh, let's walk. You've no idea how much I'm enjoying direct contact with solid ground."

They trudged in silence for a few minutes, Gray more miserable than all the stinging from his barebacked ride could account for, Sarah trying unsuccessfully to recall the more glorious sensations of balloon flight. She needed that recollection to stave off a threatening bout of the blue devils. Her instincts warned that it would be the most dampening she'd ever known.

Graymarsh spoke first. "What did you mean back there, after I'd kissed you, by 'Et tu, Brute'?"

"Did I say that? Oh, well, it's a quotation. Actresses are full of them, you know. It's from *Julius Caesar.*"

"I'm not a complete ignoramus," he said impatiently. "I know my Shakespeare—and my Latin—reasonably well. It means 'And you, Brutus?' or 'You, too, Brutus?'—something of the sort. Anyhow, Caesar said it just after the other had stuck the knife in."

"Yes. He was dismayed to find Brutus among the group," Sarah said sadly.

"So what exactly did *you* mean?"

"You know perfectly well."

"Perhaps. I'm not quite sure, though. Suppose you tell me."

She sighed. "You had just told me you loved me, you recall. You, the seventh Baron of Graymarsh, said that."

"Sixth," he corrected.

"You, the *sixth* Baron of Graymarsh, then. Titled—well, that's redundant—privileged, born with a silver spoon in your mouth, kowtowed to. That you should love Sarah Romney, out-of-work actress, of doubtful parentage, no beauty, questionable charm . . . Well, it doesn't make much sense, now does it?"

"It doesn't have to. Besides, you can scratch the part about no beauty and questionable charm. You've got that wrong."

"Thank you. To be candid, I threw it in hoping you'd disagree. It was chivalrous of you. The thing is, though"—she concentrated on the narrow path that led them out of the meadow to the carriage lane—"in spite of the absurdity of it all, when you said 'I love you' back there, I probably would have believed you—we do tend to believe what we wish to, do we not?—if the words hadn't had such a familiar ring. You see, you are the third gentleman of quality to have spoken them to me since I came to Pether Hall. And even if I had not finally discovered the plot concerning me, I don't think I'm sufficiently convinced of my own worth to have swallowed so much coincidence. Even you must admit it puts a bit of strain upon credulity. I'm only sorry to have discovered you are part of the conspiracy. You see"—she raised her head for the first time to look at him and her clear, sad gaze seemed to pierce him to the soul—"I had hoped that you were not."

The shame and misery in Gray's face was all the confirmation of his guilt that Sarah needed. Not that she could any longer doubt that he was a party to the infamous wager. Still, she longed to take his word for it when he said, "I don't suppose you'd believe it if I told you I'm not involved, wanted no part of the thing, in fact?"

Instead, she shook her head. "It doesn't stand to reason, does it? Especially after the Portsmouth inn episode. You were almost the winner, were you not, before the competition even started?"

"Who told you about the 'competition,' as you call it?" he asked bitterly. "You weren't supposed to find out. Ever. Then you couldn't have been hurt by it."

"That's a notion only a man could come up with."

"Well, some women might consider themselves fortunate in a similar situation."

She whirled on him, eyes blazing. "Sir! How dare you! I find that disgusting. *Droit du seigneur*, I suppose. Nothing is to be denied a gentleman of rank."

"I don't find that antiquated term at all appropriate," he countered, angered at an attack he felt was unjust. They trudged in silence for a little longer. Then when he was forced to jump a hedgerow—very gingerly—and reached back to lift her over, she could not free herself from his touch quickly enough.

"What are you going to do about it?" he asked abruptly as they walked on.

"Do? Why, leave Pether Hall as soon as possible. I've never walked out on a performance before in my life. It's a source of pride—actresses do have pride, you know—with me. But since the theatricals were merely a pretext to get me here—well, I no longer feel that professional standards need apply. I don't think Lady Petherbridge will mind our leaving."

Gray looked alarmed. "My aunt knows nothing of this, you understand. And is not supposed to know."

"You need not think I'd tell her such a shameful thing," Sarah retorted hotly.

"You could be tempted. I wouldn't blame you overmuch. I just wanted you to know that it would wound her deeply."

"You're a fine one to lecture me! I'm aware of her ladyship's sensibilities. Indeed, believe it or not, they are not really so different from that of any right-thinking person, regardless of class."

Even if Gray could have dredged up a reply to quell so much righteous indignation, he had no chance to deliver it. A landau appeared over a furrowed rise, bouncing precariously cross-country. Randolph, holding the reins, stood upright to his peril and hallooed at them.

The trip back to the hall was made in a strained silence that Randolph incorrectly attributed to the ordeal of flight

Sarah had just been through and Gray's guilt over being the cause of it. They soon overtook Tidswell, who had directed Randolph on his rescue mission. The Prodigy had climbed off the nag's back none too soon and was leading it, walking slightly spraddle-legged.

They reached the stableyard to find the group that had watched the unauthorized ascension collected in an anxious knot. The crowd had spied the balloon a bit before, the merest speck, heading toward the channel, and so had feared the worst. A wild cheer, in which even the ailing Lady Stanhope participated, went up when its former passengers arrived safe and sound. Miss Crome burst into tears and ran to throw her arms around Miss Romney as she alighted from the carriage. And Lord Petherbridge was moved to pat the actress on the shoulder and in a choked voice keep repeating, "Oh, I say! Oh, I say!" Indeed, the only person who appeared unmoved by the miraculous deliverance was Lady Scriven. All her attention was focused on the fact that Mr. Langford was at least as touched by Miss Crome's unseemly outburst as the beauty's mama was displeased.

The group moved together toward the hall. Lady Petherbridge decreed that Miss Romney and the Prodigy should be dosed with bark mixture and put to bed, a remedy sure to combat any resulting ill effects of balloon flight. Miss Romney did not demur, but did ask for a private word with her hostess, at her ladyship's convenience.

Gray overheard the request and pulled Randolph aside. "We need to talk to Uncle right away. Pry Gerry loose from La Scriven's clutches and go to Petherbridge's bedchamber. I'll bring the old gentleman."

While Randolph attempted to carry out this mission, Lady Petherbridge visited Sarah's room and found her packing. The actress had badly misjudged her ladyship's reaction to their leaving. She was quite upset. Nor did her attitude improve when Sarah made it clear that she'd no intention of accepting payment for the time already devoted to the play. Instead, Lady Petherbridge drew herself up to a considerable height and looked down her nose. "The money was never at issue," she said haughtily.

"I beg your ladyship's pardon. I realize it's shabby of me to abandon the play that was to have entertained your guests. But perhaps now that Lady Scriven is here, she could read my part. The rest of the cast is sufficiently prepared to carry on, I'm sure."

"Oh, bother the play!" Lady Petherbridge dismissed *The Gamester* with a wave of the hand. "It's your little brother's recitation I'm concerned with. Do you realize, young woman, that Tidswell has committed to memory the most meaningful passages from Hannah More's great work?" Her eyes glowed with a fanatic light. "What a genius that young man is!"

"T-Tidswell?"

"Tidswell!" Lady Petherbridge sat down suddenly upon a japanned couch and motioned Sarah to join her. "I will have to make a confession, Miss Romney. When I asked your brother to accompany you here, it was with the intention of opening new horizons for him. I felt it wrong that one so young should be embroiled in such a dissolute profession." If Sarah bridled just a bit, her ladyship took no notice. "And so I meant to open up new avenues to him. Show him the value of honest work—tanning, blacksmithing, farming, whatever. But then when I had your brother recite *The Merchant of Venice* for me, I saw the error of my ways."

"You did?"

"Indeed. The lad's talent is truly prodigious." Her expression was reminiscent of Mr. Adolphus Romney. "So instead of putting this light underneath a bushel, my plan was to beam it in another direction entirely." She paused, perhaps awaiting congratulations, but Sarah was struck dumb. "Now you tell me that my guests are to miss the opportunity of hearing the words of that great moralist spoken by the innocent lips of a true child prodigy. For shame, Miss Romney. For shame!"

Sarah wilted underneath her ladyship's censorious eye. "Perhaps Tids *could* stay," she offered feebly, then quickly added as her ladyship's expression brightened, "Of course, that would be entirely up to him. And really I am not at all sure that he will do it."

But whether Tidswell was too overawed by her ladyship to cross her, or too flattered that for the first time in memory someone shared his father's assessment of his talents, or too covetous of the fee that Sarah was prepared to forgo—for whatever reason, the Prodigy agreed to stay behind to perform while his sister returned alone to Portsmouth. He went to her bedchamber and told her so.

"That's really noble of you, Tids." Sarah's eyes misted. "Papa will be so proud of you and so pleased that it was you they wanted all along. But are you sure you'll be all right alone?"

"Oh, I won't be alone. I can go to Gray if I need advice." His face clouded. "At least I could have done till I lost his balloon. But anyhow," he rallied, "it's only a few more days. Beats me why you can't stick it. I've rather learned to like this life."

Much to her surprise, Sarah laughed. A few moments before, she had thought never to laugh again. "Oh, Tids," she choked, "don't get too comfortable among the nobs. You're letting yourself in for a terrible come-down."

"That's as may be." Her little brother looked resolute. "How much does that Kean fellow make in a year at Drury Lane?"

"Barely enough to keep Lord Petherbridge in horses. Loath as I am to burst your bubble, dear Tidswell, I fear you have to be born into a life like this."

Master Romney heaved a regretful sigh.

Chapter Sixteen

The meeting in progress in another part of Pether Hall was not proceeding half as smoothly as the tête-à-tête between Lady Petherbridge and Miss Romney. Lord Petherbridge had taken a wide-legged stance in front of his bedchamber fireplace and was glaring at his three nephews, who were seated like errant schoolboys in front of him. "What a bunch of nincompoops you three turned out to be. I never would have proposed this scheme if I'd thought you'd make such a shocking mull of it. It seemed simple enough. Practically any cove I know could have brought the thing about. And one of you ought to have been able to get the girl to marry you. Why, a penniless actress should jump at the chance to wed a man-about-town. But no—somebody here had to go spill out the whole story and get the girl's hackles up. And next thing you know, she'll be telling tales to Augusta. Dammit, most likely she already has!"

"No, she won't do that," Gray said.

"Fustian. Never knew a female to hold her tongue."

"Miss Romney said she was not going to tell our aunt and we can depend upon her to keep her word. Which is more than can be said for one gentleman present."

"What's that supposed to mean?" Randolph bristled.

"Yes, Cousin, before you begin your accusations, you might stop to consider that you're the one who's discussed the matter with Miss Romney. You can hardly be considered free of suspicion yourself, you know."

"Stop your wrangling!" Lord Petherbridge commanded in a terrible voice. "We ain't got time to discover who the tattler is. The thing is, what's to be done? The girl's leaving."

"Well, if you wish my opinion . . ." Gerard paused, apparently not considering the present dilemma as important as his snuff-taking ritual.

"Of course I wish it. I just asked for it, didn't I?" Lord Petherbridge glared while his nephew inhaled.

"Well, then, I think you should simply call Miss Romney in and make a clean breast of the whole thing. Evidently, the girl thinks she's been made a fool of. Here she thought we were pursuing her for herself alone, then she finds out there's a fortune involved. From one point of view, I suppose it is rather humiliating. But when she calms down a bit, I think she'll come to realize that feeling a trifle foolish is a small price to pay for going from rags to riches. She's a sensible girl. She'll respect your wish to keep your relationship a secret. She'll not want to upset Aunt Augusta—be a blot on the family escutcheon or whatever. Explain to her that part about wanting your own flesh and blood—a rather grisly term for offspring, don't you think?—here at Pether Hall. She'll come about. And then . . ." He paused again while they all waited.

"Well!" Lord Petherbridge barked. "Then *what*?"

"Why, then, let *her* choose one of us."

"But, you sap-skull," Randolph said, giving him a disgusted look, "she's already turned us down."

"In the heat of the moment. A feminine reaction to discovering that her fortune weighed more heavily in our eyes than she did. Actually, it's a pity that the whole thing wasn't lined out for her in the beginning. I'm sure she would have been ecstatic. It's only this duplicity that's sent her up into the boughs."

"By George, you may be right." His uncle looked at the Corinthian with new respect.

"Of course I am. Call her in and let her choose."

"She could even draw straws." The suggestion came from Randolph, who did not think too highly of his prospects.

"What do you say, Gray?" Lord Petherbridge turned his protuberant gaze on Lord Graymarsh, who merely shrugged.

"That ain't exactly helpful," his uncle retorted. "But if no one's got a better plan, we'll talk to the girl. No use having her go off in a pucker. Might turn her even more stubborn." His mind made up, he gave the bell a pull and dispatched Mason to summon Miss Romney to the library. The three young men seemed to take that as a signal for departure and rose hastily to their feet.

"Sit!" his lordship barked in a tone usually reserved for his pet spaniel. "You ain't leaving me in the lurch. One of you is responsible for mucking up a perfectly good scheme for the continuation of the Petherbridge line, and by gad you'll stay here and help me put things to rights."

As a result of Petherbridge's exhortation to the troops, Sarah found all four gentlemen seated around the library table with the lord of the manor at its head and, for fortification, a port decanter at his elbow. Pausing on the threshold, her first inclination at the sight of her three dishonorable suitors was to turn on her heel and leave. But as the gentlemen all stood, Lord Petherbridge looked so perturbed that out of civility to her host, who certainly had intended her no harm, she made herself walk toward them.

"Do come sit down, Miss Romney." His lordship gestured to the chair at the foot of the table, which Mr. Langford was holding for her. "Didn't want you to leave in a pucker. Wouldn't be right. You're owed some kind of explanation."

Sarah struggled for composure. "Really, your lordship, I'd rather not discuss the matter, if you don't mind."

"Oh, but I say, m'dear, you have to let me try to set things right, you know. Wouldn't be the thing not to explain."

Sarah relented. Although her greatest wish was to forget all about the demeaning wager and get on with her life, she was touched by the fact that Lord Petherbridge was so upset over his nephews' odious behavior. If he wished to try and smooth things over, well, for his sake, she'd be civil. She accepted the chair that Gerard pulled out without looking at him or at either of his cousins.

The gaze that Lord Petherbridge then bent upon her was awash with emotion. Annoyance, embarrassment, befuddlement—all warred within him. Annoyance won.

"I have to tell you," he began abruptly, "I ain't at all pleased with these three nephews of mine."

"I did not think you would be, my lord," she replied with quiet dignity.

"Bungled the thing. Made a complete mull of it. I should have thought that any one of 'em could have brought the thing about. Nothing to it, really."

Sarah stared at the old gentleman, stunned and appalled. Surely she had misunderstood what he'd just said. "You cannot mean, Lord Petherbridge, that you actually knew what these 'gentlemen' were up to."

"Of course I knew. Had to, didn't I?" he said impatiently. "It was me own idea, naturally."

Again Sarah almost rejected the testimony of her own ears. They must have played her false. She was actually more shocked by this elderly gentleman's disclosure than by the knavish behavior of the younger men. And she hardly trusted herself not to throw the inkpot before her at any one of the family group. Instead, she rose from the table, bent on stalking from the room. Her voice shook with righteous indignation. "You, sir, should be thoroughly ashamed of yourself."

"Ashamed of myself? Well, I say now, that's cutting it a bit rough." His lordship had the hurt look of a spanked puppy.

"Rough? I beg to differ. In view of your shocking disclosure, I consider my reaction quite restrained."

"For the life of me, can't see why you call it shocking. I'll not say what I did was quite the thing, but it ain't all that unusual. And not to put too fine a point on it, it ain't as if I forced your mother. Or didn't pay for your upkeep, when it comes to that."

There really was something terribly wrong with her hearing. Or perhaps her wits were the real culprit. Since she'd walked through the library door, nothing seemed to be making any sense. Now she felt her knees grow weak, a prelude to comprehension. Sarah sat back down, her face drained of color.

Gray, who had been watching her intently, spoke up. His voice was gentle. "Sarah, what did you think this was all about? All of us dangling after you, I mean."

"I thought it was a wager," she managed to say. "Randolph—somebody—said that it was common practice. For gentlemen to bet on which of them could seduce a certain female first. That was the idea, wasn't it?"

"Oh, dear God." Gray groaned.

"You muttonheads!" Petherbridge thundered. "You had

the lass here thinking that all you wanted was a tumble in the hay! Of all the pea-brains I ever heard of . . ." he sputtered, and words failed.

"I did no such thing," Randolph protested. "I made her an honorable offer. Even said I loved her."

"I think we both—all?—said that," Gerard commented. "But I collect that Miss Romney here merely took our declarations for moonshine to cloak our less honorable intentions. Did you not, Miss Romney?"

Sarah, who could no longer persuade her vocal chords to work, merely nodded.

"Well, of all the bungling idiots! Of all the sap-skulled cloth-heads!" Lord Petherbridge began his diatribe again, then just as suddenly calmed down. "Can't be helped, though. See now I was a fool. Should have made a clean breast of the whole thing to you from the start, Miss Romney—Sarah, I mean to say. But I didn't know you then, you see. Now that I've been in your company awhile, well"—he choked suddenly with emotion—"I'd just like to say that I couldn't be prouder if you'd been, well, uh, born on the right side of the blanket." He had a bit of trouble interpreting her look. "You do understand now that I'm your natural father?" She nodded, and he continued. "Well, now that I've seen for myself the kind of girl you are, I realize I could have trusted you not to let the cat out of the bag. Wouldn't do, you understand. Augusta's a very straitlaced woman. She wouldn't take kindly to me early, uh, indiscretions. But I should have told you right off that I want you to have me fortune. My only child, don't you see. But since I can't just will it to you in the ordinary way of things, I told these three I'd leave it to whichever one of them succeeded in marrying you. With you none the wiser as to why."

At this point, Miss Romney shifted her gaze from his lordship's face to look at each of his nephews in turn. The beautiful eyes remained fixed especially long on Graymarsh, who turned a deep, dark red.

"That's still the only way to handle things. Except now you'll know what's what. Well, then. I think we can just forget the courtship, which they don't have the slightest notion of how to go about, anyhow, and let you choose. Tell me, girl, which one of me nephews will you have?"

With great difficulty, Sarah pulled herself together. "Do I understand you right, sir? I will inherit your fortune if I marry one of these 'gentlemen'?"

"That's it." By now, Petherbridge was enjoying his fairy-godfather role. The girl was obviously overcome by the miracle of it all. "At least that's the gist of the business. Like I told you, you can't be named in me will. Wouldn't do, you understand. So it's your husband who'll do the inheriting. Comes to the same thing in the end. All you need to do is decide which of 'em it's to be."

"That's all?" she asked softly.

"I'll grant you it's a bit of a poser. Gray's me choice, I don't mind saying. Think he'd make you the best husband. But then, of course, Gerard's better-looking. Females set store by that sort of thing. And he needs me money more. As does Randolph," Lord Petherbridge added in the interest of fair play. "He's a good-enough lad, too. So which one will it be, girl?"

Again Miss Romney gave each gentleman an appraising glance. "As you say, your lordship," she then replied with a coolness that surprised her, "the problem is a poser. There is not, after all, a great deal to choose among them. I agree that Mr. Langford's need is greatest. His debts, I understand, are enormous. He's prepared, it seems, to go to any lengths to settle them. Any, that is, except to earn an honest living. He is, however, quite prepared to see the woman he loves sold to the highest bidder. And, as a last resort, to sell himself to Lady Scriven, whom he positively dislikes. It must have seemed very attractive, Mr. Langford, to have the opportunity to marry me, to whom you are merely indifferent. Especially since you would be able to control the purse strings, a thing impossible in Lady Scriven's case, I collect. Besides, I'm given to understand that Lord Petherbridge's fortune puts the widow's to shame. Is that not so?" Mr. Langford, whose composure was wearing thin, merely nodded. "So that puts me in the running well ahead of Lady Scriven. And leaves Miss Crome, the sentimental favorite, a distant third.

"As for Randolph, did you realize, your lordship, that he has a passion for the land? Not to teach you your own business, sir, but you really should be backing him to win me. He'd be the one who'd increase your holdings and turn your estate into an agricultural showplace. No wonder he was so eager to press his suit. His motives, at any rate, are not to be despised."

She paused a bit before continuing. "As for your choice, Lord Graymarsh—well, I understand he's at least as wealthy as you. But as King Midas demonstrated, one never seems to feel quite rich enough. So I expect greed was the emotion behind his lordship's pursuit."

"Oh, I say!" Randolph protested, observing the look on his brother's face. "It ain't fair to call Gray greedy. He never wanted any part of this business from the first."

"Never mind, Randolph. You're wasting your breath," Graymarsh said quietly.

"I think you wrong your nephews, Lord Petherbridge," Miss Romney said, ignoring the interruption, "by thinking they made a mull of things. Indeed, their courtships were all that one might reasonably have hoped for. They each had a great deal to gain and each gave the chase his best. Perhaps if I've failed to point out the lengths to which they were prepared to go to achieve their ends, it's because the language itself is lacking. If only there were some good term to describe the male of the species who prostitutes himself for money, you'd get the picture instantly. What an odd oversight, come to think of it, when our vocabulary is so rich with descriptions for the grasping female: Venus mendicant, lightskirt, bit o' muslin, fashionable impure . . . Oh, I do like that one especially! Fashionable impure. Now that label could do for either sex, don't you agree?"

"Oh, I say . . . Come now! Really, Miss Romney," Lord Petherbridge sputtered, "you go too far! There's no comparison between the, er, activities of the sort of female you refer to and this situation. I think you owe me nephews an apology. Except for the fact you didn't happen to know you were me heir, there's nothing unusual in this sort of arrangement. It's done all the time."

"I realize that. But I still maintain that the practice of selling one's self for money is a custom shared by the upper classes and the ladies of the evening. The rest of us, thank goodness, are able to choose our mates for love. That makes me the only free person in this room." She got to her feet. "Now, if you gentlemen will excuse me."

"B-but," his lordship expostulated, "you can't go yet. You ain't said which one of 'em you'll have."

"Oh, have I still not made it clear? I beg pardon, my lord. I thought you understood that I would not marry one of your nephews at gunpoint."

"But you have to!" Lord Petherbridge also stood. "I thought *you* understood. You can't inherit unless you do."

"Oh, I understand that right enough. But what your lordship fails to grasp is that I wish nothing from you. I know you mean well by me, sir, but your concern is quite misplaced. You see, I'm already an heiress. My *father*"—she stressed the word—"plans to leave the thing he values most, the Romney Company of Players, in my charge. So if you'll excuse me, I'm going home to help him get my inheritance back on its feet."

"Young woman, have you gone daft?" his lordship roared. "Do you understand what it is you're being offered? You can't know that you're whistling a fortune down the wind for the chance to work with a bunch of broken-down, third-rate, talentless actors!'' Words failed him as Sarah started toward the door.

''I resent your name-calling, but never mind,'' she answered over her shoulder. ''In reply to your question, I know exactly what I'm doing.''

''My God!'' His lordship stared at his nephews. ''The girl's queer in the attic. I don't know what to say.''

The actress broke her exit with one hand resting on the doorknob. She turned to gaze with pity at his lordship. ''That, sir, underscores the difference between you and my real father—the one who loved and reared me. He is never at a loss for words. May I suggest that were he in your place—though, given our relationship, such a similar situation would not arise—but, hypothetically, if it did, he'd borrow this phrase from *Lear*: 'How sharper than a serpent's tooth it is to have a thankless child.' ''

Adolphus Romney himself could not have topped her reading. Well satisfied with the dramatic climax, Miss Romney closed the door behind her.

The four men stood in silence, looking at one another. ''I tell you the girl's queer in the attic,'' his lordship repeated. ''Madder than old King George. Throwing me fortune back in me face that way. I tell you, there's bad blood there. Goes to show, lads. Don't pay to get yourself involved with cits. Stark, raving mad! And just what she thinks a bunch of toothless serpents have to say in the matter defies all understanding. Queer in the attic. Got to be. It's the only explanation.''

Chapter Seventeen

Lords Petherbridge and Graymarsh, the Honorable Randolph Milbanke, and Mr. Gerard Langford had drained the port decanter when Mr. Langford pushed back his chair from the library table and rose rather unsteadily to his feet. "Well, I for one am going to dress for dinner. Or should I say make myself 'fashionable.' Coming, fellow 'impures'?"

"That ain't funny," Randolph retorted. "I can't think what got into Sarah to say such a maggoty thing about us. 'Fashionable impures,' indeed! I didn't like it above half."

"Yes, but you must admit it was 'a hit, a very palpable hit.' You see, Miss Romney isn't the only one who can spout Shakespeare. Coming, Gray?"

"In a moment. I'd like a word with his lordship first."

As the library door closed behind his brother and cousin,

Gray turned to Lord Petherbridge, who was slumped down in his chair, staring morosely at the empty decanter. "I know my timing is poor," he said gently, "but since I plan to leave right away, I think we should discuss your will."

"Trying to steal a march on the other two, are you? My God, the chit was right. You are greedy."

"Perhaps. But not in this instance. I'm not about to suggest that you make me your heir."

"You ain't? Well, then, I hope you ain't planning to try to talk me into leaving something for that—that *actress*, for I won't do it. Most ungrateful female I—"

"No, I'm not going to suggest that either," Gray broke in. "Given her prejudice against being pursued for her fortune, I'm not eager for her to be an heiress. You see, I intend to marry Sarah."

"You what! Have you taken leave of your senses? The girl's a shrew! A termagant! Besides," Petherbridge added more practically, "she just said she wouldn't have you."

"That is a leveler," Gray admitted. "But once she realizes my motives aren't mercenary, I think I can bring her about."

"Don't see why you'd want to. She's queer in the attic, I tell you."

"Oh, I don't think so. A bit overly dramatic, perhaps. That's to be expected. And her background makes her look at things from a different perspective than we're used to—not such a bad thing, really," he mused. "Then, too, I suspect she's inherited an overdose of Petherbridge pride."

"Petherbridge pride? Oh, I say." His lordship perked up a bit. "By Jove, do you think so?"

"Of course. Blood will tell, you know."

"Hmmm. Hadn't thought of that. Well, now, I collect there may be something in what you say. The chit does look a bit like me sister Fanny, come to think on it. And, God knows, Fanny was a great one for flying up into the boughs over the least little thing. Humph! Can't say I'm as keen on the notion as I once was, but, well, if you do persuade the girl to marry you, I expect I might reconsider and leave you me blunt as agreed on."

"No! No!" Gray almost shouted. "That's just what you are not to do! My God, my life will be intolerable if you name me in your will. The girl will never believe she was all I ever wanted. Which brings us to the matter I wished to discuss with you. Would you consider dividing your inheritance between Gerard and Randolph?"

Lord Graymarsh went on to outline his plan. "Leave Gerry the townhouse and all your assets outside of the estate. And if you could see your way clear to settling his debts right away, sir, then he could go ahead and marry Miss Crome on his prospects."

"Marry Miss Crome! Ridiculous! You've let yourself be gulled by that actress's ravings. An out-and-outer like Gerry shackled to a schoolroom miss? To a female who has the vapors every time you look at her at that? Preposterous! Makes no sense at all."

"Oh, I couldn't agree more, sir. But he does seem to love her."

"Why, he'd never be able to stomach Lady Emma Crome for a stepmama. Know I couldn't."

"Again I agree. But then Gerry should have to pay something for his sins. Will you think about it?"

"I'll consider naming the lad in me will, but I don't believe for a minute he'll be sap-skulled enough to wed a penniless chit with a harpy for a mama. He can't be such a green 'un after all these years."

"Well, you could be right, sir. Now about Randolph—"

"You're taking a lot on yourself, ain't you, nevvy?"

"Well, yes, but I trust in no way you'll object to. My next suggestion is that you leave the estate to Randolph. And let him know it. But, most important, give him the running of it now. It will keep him occupied for the many years your lordship should still enjoy. And I don't think you'll regret it. The lad really does know what's what when it comes to farming."

"I'll think on it." Lord Petherbridge sounded grudging, but had, in fact, already begun mulling things over in his mind. "Can't expect me to come up with an answer now. There's been too much hubble-bubble already for one day. First that curst balloon of yours taking off with those actors aboard. Then me own little Sarah turning into a—what did she call it? A toothless child? Well, really, Gray, I think it's a bit much for you to be settling the terms of me will right now."

"I know, sir," the young man said soothingly. "Rotten timing, and I do beg pardon for it. Just let me point out, though, that when the dust settles, things should work out fairly close to the way you've always planned. Only instead of the three of us nephews inheriting—I'm speaking now of your original scheme—it will be a two-way thing. And even though your own flesh and blood won't be actually living at Pether Hall, well, they'll be in and out of here all the time if I've anything to say in the matter. So all's well that ends well. My God! Is that the bard, too? The curst habit's catching."

He pushed back his chair. "I shouldn't keep you. You'll need to dress. I'll say my good-byes now, sir. I won't be staying."

"Oh? Going after the girl now, are you?"

"Oh, Lord, no. In her present temper, I wouldn't dare. No, I think Miss Romney will need a nice, long cooling-off period."

"So why not eat your mutton? No need to go rushing off."

"Oh, I'm afraid I have rather urgent business in town, my lord." Gray grinned. "You see, I have to see some men about a new balloon."

* * *

The Romney Company of Players was experiencing a turnabout in fortune. Adolphus Romney had found a backer for them—due entirely, so he said, to Tidswell's connections with the aristocracy. "Once it was learned, m'dear," he explained to Sarah, "that the Prodigy had been engaged for a solo performance at Pether Hall, well, there was simply no scarcity of gentlemen eager to finance us. Our success is assured."

As usual, Sarah made allowances for exaggeration. But she didn't look the gift horse of a change of luck too closely in the mouth. She gratefully accepted the opportunity to immerse herself in work.

The company planned to reopen with *The Gamester*, with Sarah in the female lead. If the associations of that drama were somewhat painful, this drawback was outweighed by the fact that its small cast fit their dwindled company. And since Sarah had already learned her part, she could give more attention to other aspects of production, such as the playbills.

Mr. Romney had bespoken a ridiculous number of these broadsides. Sarah tried to remonstrate over the expense, then sighed and capitulated as he chided, "Think big, m'dear, think big."

Just how big the manager's thoughts on publicity had grown became abundantly clear when Sarah and Tids were on the way to the theater for dress rehearsal. They hurried across the cobbled street, with Tidswell talking a mile a minute about an improvement he had made in their wind machine, when suddenly he froze and clutched Sarah's arm while an outraged voice behind them roared, "Look out!"

Adjusting their position slightly so that a covered cart could go around them while its driver muttered curses, Tids pointed skyward. "Look up there, Sarah, would you?"

Her chip-straw bonnet being inadequate to the task, Sarah shaded her eyes with her hand against the sun. But even while squinting into the glare, she had no trouble indentifying the blurred object that bobbed their way. "It's a balloon," she remarked brilliantly.

"By George, you don't suppose!"

"Don't be ridiculous. His is in France by now, in case you've forgotten."

"Well, the wind could have changed," Tids muttered.

"Get out of the street, you numbskulls!" a gentleman in a phaeton yelled. The two obliged him. "Come on, Tids. We'll be late."

"I don't care. I want to see it." Tids planted himself in front of a draper's shop. Sarah glared, then sighed and took up a position next to him.

The balloon was close enough now for easy identification. The silk was a bright, bold yellow, banded with zigzag stripes of blue, the colors borrowed from sun and sky to appear at home in the alien heavens. "Oh, it's lovely," Sarah breathed, while her brother muttered, "Rats! I'd hoped—"

The craft was descending rapidly now, heading down over the High Street. "Oh, goodness, it's going to crash!" Sarah exclaimed.

"No such thing!" Tids yipped. "Look at that, would you!" A shower of leaflets came drifting down from the dangling basket as the balloon floated above their heads close enough for the lone aeronaut to be identified. "It is Gray!" Tidswell whooped, while Sarah's knees grew weak. A piece of paper drifted past her face and she automatically reached out and clutched it. "Portsmouth Theatre!!!" the broadside proclaimed in big, bold print. "This present Monday, July 15, 1816, the Romney Players will present—"

There was more, a whole sheet's worth, in fact, but Sarah never got to read it. "Come on!" Tidswell dragged her along in the wake of the balloon and amid the rushing company of every pedestrian and horse-drawn vehicle in sight. "By Jove, Gray plans to land in the park!" he shouted to her.

"Does he, indeed?" She panted. "Well, then, we'd best look for it anywhere. The church spire seems a likely spot."

But this time Sarah had unjustly maligned Lord Graymarsh's navigational skills. After hovering for some minutes over the grassy open space while he rained leaflets upon the gathering crowd, Gray descended among thunderous applause for a perfect landing. "Tids, help me!" he shouted as the Prodigy came bounding up.

Sarah stood on the fringes of the crowd, willing herself to leave but quite unable to do so as the two, with some volunteer help from several spectators, scrambled to make the balloon secure.

Once this thing had been accomplished, Lord Graymarsh declaimed with all the assurance and authority of centuries of breeding, "Ladies and gentlemen, may I present one of the stars of the internationally famous Romney Company? Here he is, Master Tidswell Romney—better known to his adoring public as *the Prodigy*!"

The crowd broke into noisy, if somewhat mystified, cheers and clapping. "Just tell 'em about the play, Tids," Gray whispered soothingly as the boy looked around him for an avenue of escape. The Prodigy gulped twice, took a monstrous breath, then launched into a spiel touting the merits of *The Gamester*. Gray waited till the lad was caught up in his own oratory, then pushed through the crowd toward Miss Romney.

" *'Deus ex machina.'* " She looked up at him wonderingly.

"You do have a quotation for every occasion, don't you, love?" His smile was tender. " 'The God from the machine'? Well, I've been called worse things. Even by you."

Sarah managed to wrench her attention away from the warmth of his eyes to ask, "But what are you doing here?"

"Besides the obvious? Well, in addition to publicizing *The Gamester*, I plan to operate the fog machine. It's all in aid of protecting my investment. I'm your new backer. Didn't Adolphus tell you?"

"No, he did not!" She found the revelation humiliating. "But then I should have known," she added grimly.

"Indeed, you should have. As you pointed out when you rang a peal over us all at Pether Hall, no one of my class ever weds except for profit. And since you are heir to the Romney Company, and since it's the *only* thing you'll ever be heir to . . . Oh, by the by, I should perhaps mention that Lord Petherbridge is leaving his fortune to Randolph and Gerry. Unconditionally. They can marry whom they please, uh, as long as it's not you, that is. Our Gerry has already taken advantage of this new freedom by eloping with Miss Crome."

"Oh, has he? I'm so glad."

"I thought you might be, since it was all your doing. You've sorted us out rather well, in fact. Or you will have done, as soon as you consent to marry me."

"As soon as I what? You aren't serious, surely?"

"Never more so, I assure you."

"But you can't possibly be offering for me, can you?" She looked about her at the park, the people, the balloon, and Tidswell, who was dominating the scene in a manner that would have made his father proud. "No, that's perfectly ridiculous. Of course you can't be."

"Whyever not? It may not be a very romantic proposal: I'll grant you that. But when else will I get the chance? I'm sure you won't miss a rehearsal merely to settle your future happiness. That's too unprofessional for Miss Romney. Damn!" He snapped his fingers. "I forgot to say that I have your father's permission to address you. Making an offer's more complicated than one realizes."

"My father's permission?"

"Yes. I am, of course, referring to Mr. Adolphus Romney. Oh, everything's all quite proper in spite of my bad choice of time and place. I asked, and he approves."

She gurgled suddenly. "Y-yes. I expect he would."

"Let's see now, that should about cover everything. Oh, blast! Have I said I love you? Granted, it's a touchy phrase where you're concerned and may simply put you into another taking. But I do feel that such a declaration is essential when proposing marriage. So it's a risk I'm prepared to take."

"It's good of you to be so conscientious."

"It's true, actually. I do love you." The light in his eyes intensified as he closed the gap between them. "I'm really quite humiliatingly in love, in fact. Find myself doing the damnedest things." He looked ruefully around at the strewn leaflets all about them. "Things completely out of character. Do you know, I think I loved you from the first," he continued huskily, drawing her into his arms. "I think I even loved you right through that awful fright wig and that appalling nose."

"You couldn't possibly have done so." Her voice remained unconvinced even as her arms found their way around his neck and her face turned upward.

"Oh, yes, I could have." Just before his lips met hers, he managed to murmur, "You see, you do have the most extraordinary eyes."

Time stood still. The world retreated. They were alone. There was nothing but their love, their joy, their completeness. Nothing, that is, except a persistent, high-pitched voice in the background haranguing with an insistence that finally penetrated even love's defenses.

"Stop it, Sarah! Really, I must say! Tying your garters this way in public! It ain't at all the thing! And your lordship should be ashamed! What will Papa say?"

"Nothing, you odious brat, if you don't tell him." Graymarsh released his lady with reluctance. "Or better still," he added as the crowd, now collected around them, whistled and clapped, "just explain to your father that the two of us were doing a love scene from *The Gamester*, giving the public a brief preview."

"Was that really what you were doing?" The Prodigy looked skeptical.

"Of course. Oh, by the by, Sarah love, can I take it that your scandalous behavior means you've accepted me?"

She nodded, not yet trusting herself to speak.

"You mean you've actually asked Sarah to marry you?"

"Yes. I trust that meets with your approval."

"Meets with my approval!" The Prodigy whooped. "I should say! Well, yes, by George, it does! I say, this really is the most famous thing imaginable!"

"Well, thank you, Tidswell. I'm quite touched," the sixth Baron of Graymarsh said.

"By Jove, it's like some unbelievable play. An out-and-out fairy tale. Why, I couldn't have arranged things better if I'd had a lamp to rub, or three wishes, or a magic potion—any of that farfetched sort of thing."

"Why, thank you, Tidswell. And I'm proud, too, to have *you* for a brother."

"Brother?" The Prodigy looked blank. And then, suddenly, enlightened. "Oh, yes, I see now what you mean. The brother thing's nice, too, of course. But what I was really thinking of was how famous it's going to be to have a genuine, top-of-the-trees balloon right in the bosom of my family. How soon can we go up, sir?"

True romance is not hard to find... you need only look as far as FAWCETT BOOKS

Available at your bookstore or use this coupon.

___THE FALSE BETHROTHAL, Clarice Peters	20513	2.25
___SAMANTHA, Clarice Peters	20217	2.25
___THEA, Clarice Peters	20696	2.50
___A VERY SIMPLE SCHEME, Rebecca Baldwin	50274	1.50
___A SEASON ABROAD, Rebecca Baldwin	50215	1.50

FAWCETT MAIL SALES
Dept. TAF, 201 E. 50th St., New York, N.Y. 10022

Please send me the FAWCETT BOOKS I have checked above. I am enclosing $..................(add 50¢ per copy to cover postage and handling). Send check or money order—no cash or C.O.D.'s please. Prices and numbers are subject to change without notice. Valid in U.S. only. All orders are subject to availability of books.

Name___________________________

Address___________________________

City______________State__________Zip Code__________

Allow at least 4 weeks for delivery.

TAF-43